MARVEL ACTION
AVENGERS
OFF THE CLOCK

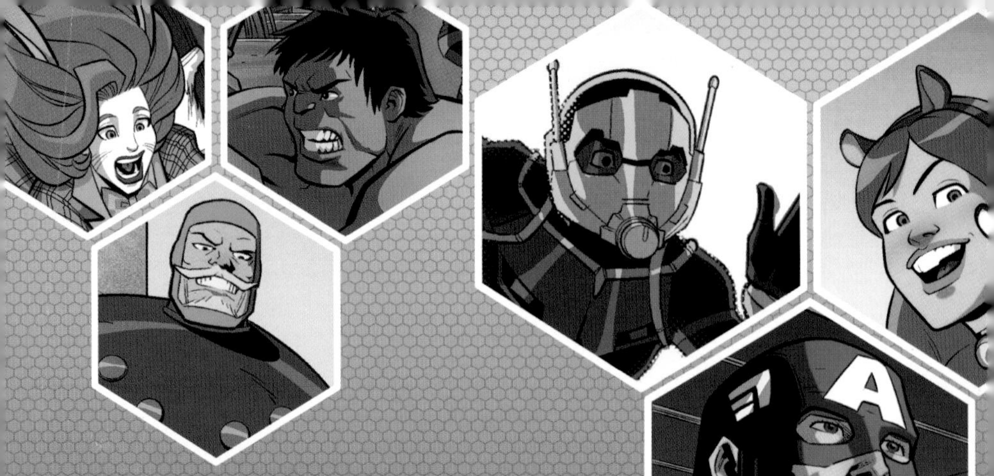

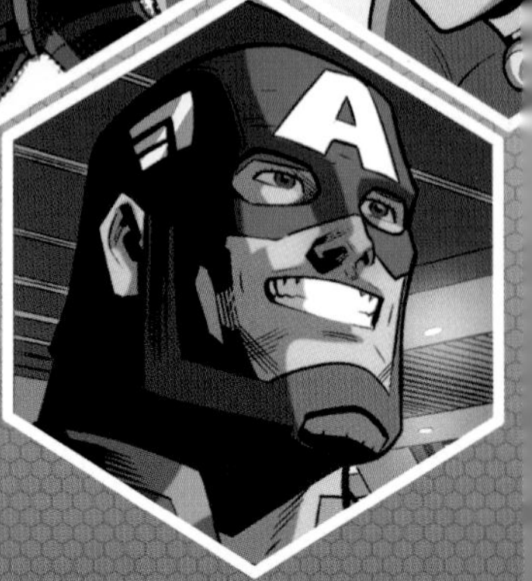

Marvel Publishing:

VP Production & Special Projects: Jeff Youngquist
Editor, Juvenile Publishing: Lauren Bisom
Assistant Editor, Special Projects: Caitlin O'Connell
VP, Licensed Publishing: Sven Larsen
SVP Print, Sales & Marketing: David Gabriel
Editor In Chief: C.B. Cebulski

IDW Publishing:

IDW

Collection Edits
ALONZO SIMON and ZAC BOONE

Production Artist
NATHAN WIDICK

Cover Artist
BUTCH MAPA

Nachie Marsham, Publisher
Rebekah Cahalin, EVP of Operations
Blake Kobashigawa, VP of Sales
John Barber, Editor-in-Chief
Mark Doyle, Editorial Director, Originals
Justin Eisinger, Editorial Director, Graphic Novels and Collections
Scott Dunbier, Director, Special Projects
Anna Morrow, Sr. Marketing Director
Tara McCrillis, Director of Design & Production
Shauna Monteforte, Sr. Director of Manufacturing Operations

Ted Adams and Robbie Robbins, IDW Founders

ISBN: 978-1-68405-729-0 24 23 22 21 1 2 3 4

Special thanks: **Tom Brevoort**

ART BY: BUTCH MAPA

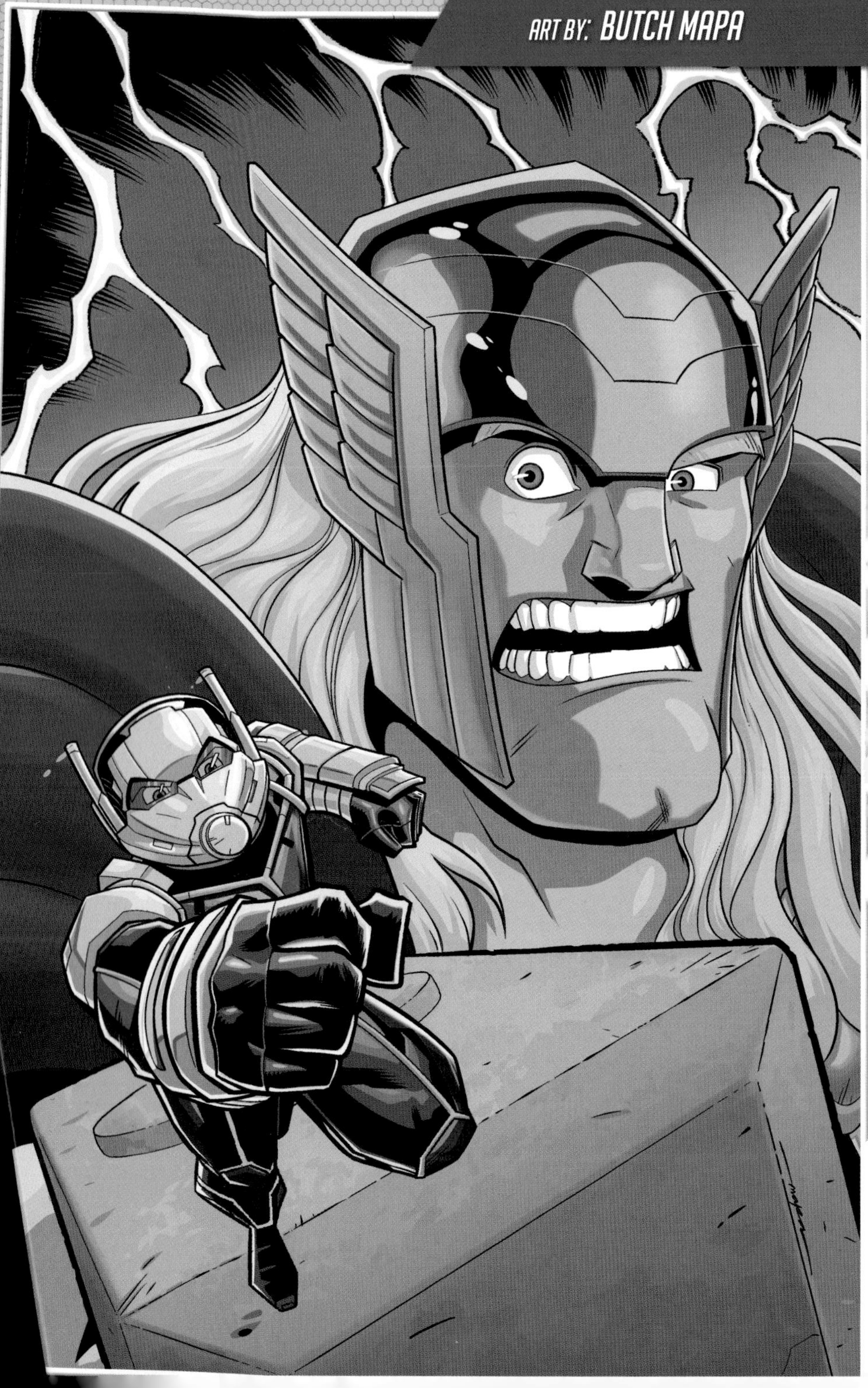

MARVEL

MARVEL ACTION AVENGERS

OFF THE CLOCK

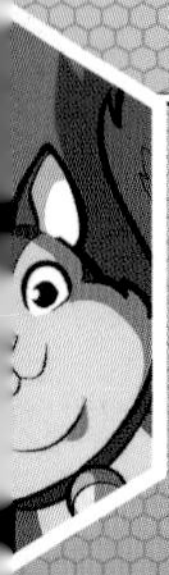

WRITTEN BY KATIE COOK

ART BY BUTCH MAPA

COLORS BY PROTOBUNKER

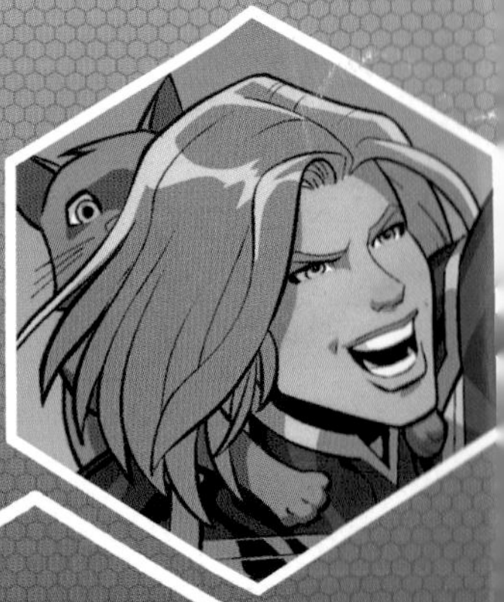

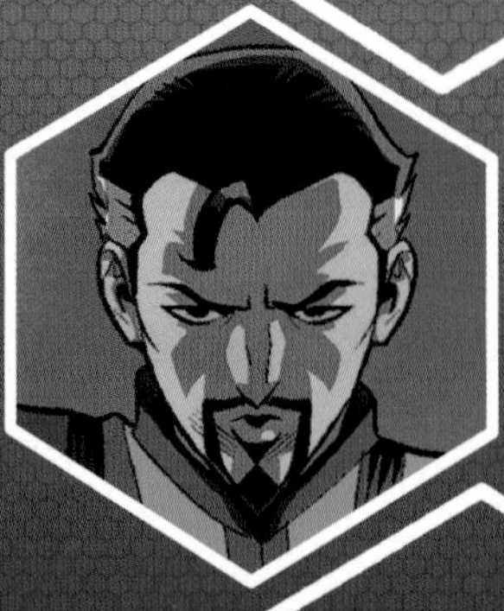

LETTERS BY CHRISTA MIESNER
AND VALERIA LOPEZ

ASSISTANT EDITS BY MEGAN BROWN

EDITED BY BOBBY CURNOW

AVENGERS CREATED BY
STAN LEE & JACK KIRBY

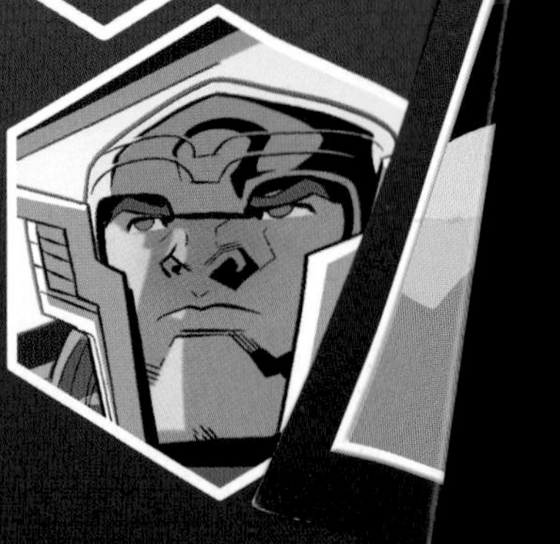

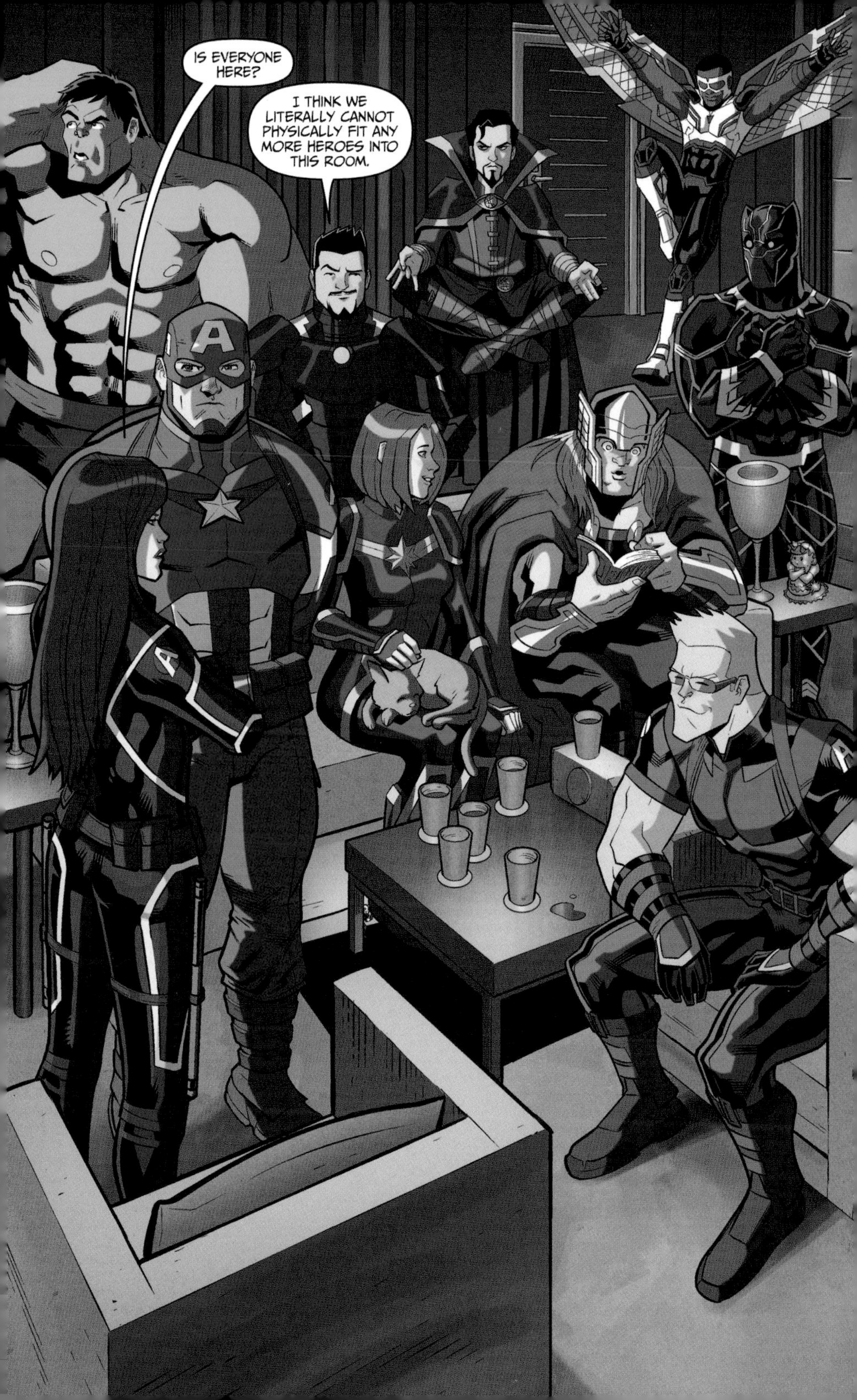
IS EVERYONE HERE?
I THINK WE LITERALLY CANNOT PHYSICALLY FIT ANY MORE HEROES INTO THIS ROOM.

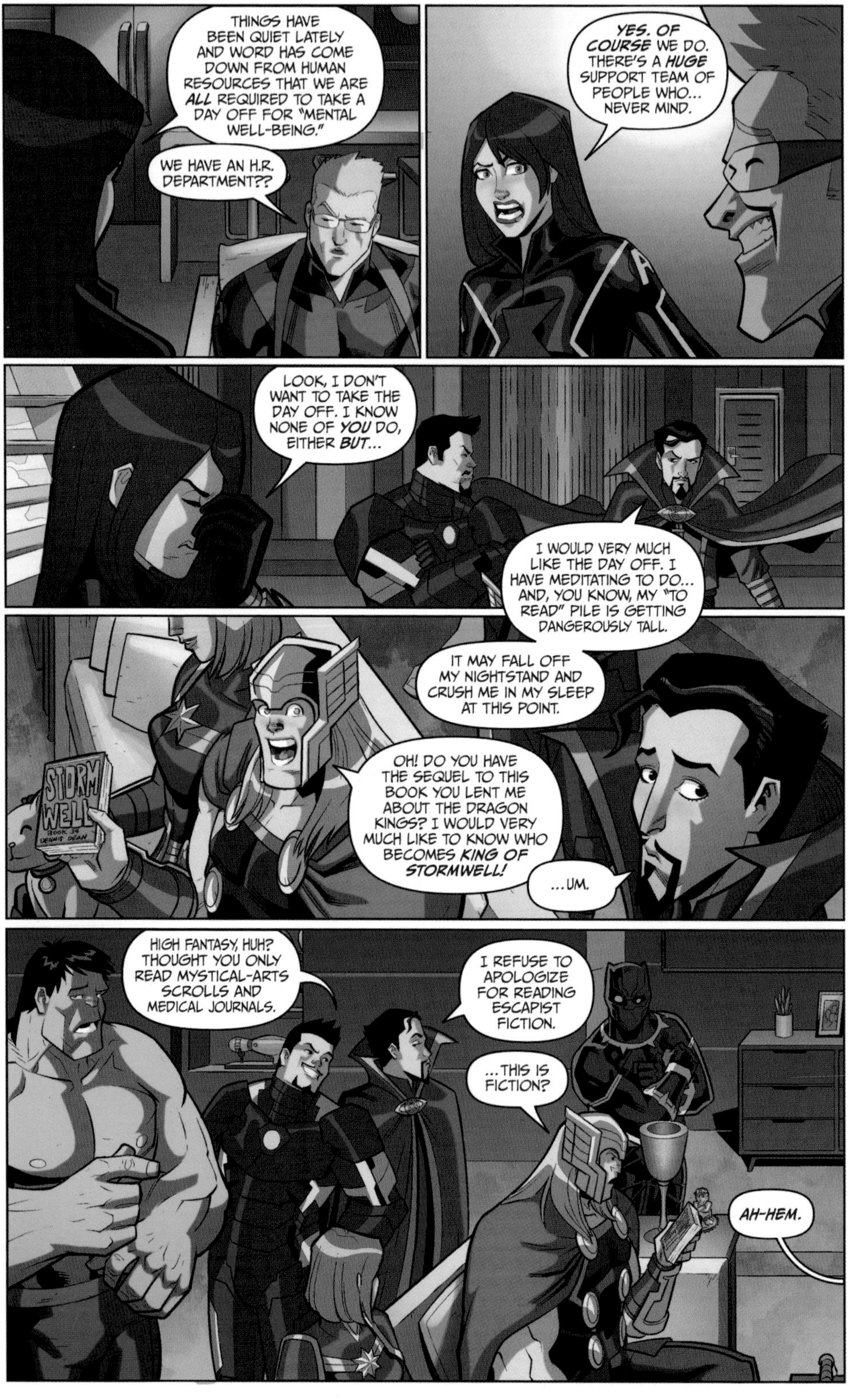
THINGS HAVE BEEN QUIET LATELY AND WORD HAS COME DOWN FROM HUMAN RESOURCES THAT WE ARE ALL REQUIRED TO TAKE A DAY OFF FOR "MENTAL WELL-BEING."
WE HAVE AN H.R. DEPARTMENT??
YES. OF COURSE WE DO. THERE'S A HUGE SUPPORT TEAM OF PEOPLE WHO... NEVER MIND.
LOOK, I DON'T WANT TO TAKE THE DAY OFF. I KNOW NONE OF YOU DO, EITHER BUT...
I WOULD VERY MUCH LIKE THE DAY OFF. I HAVE MEDITATING TO DO... AND, YOU KNOW, MY "TO READ" PILE IS GETTING DANGEROUSLY TALL.
IT MAY FALL OFF MY NIGHTSTAND AND CRUSH ME IN MY SLEEP AT THIS POINT.
STORM WELL
BOOK 34
DENNIS DEAN
OH! DO YOU HAVE THE SEQUEL TO THIS BOOK YOU LENT ME ABOUT THE DRAGON KINGS? I WOULD VERY MUCH LIKE TO KNOW WHO BECOMES KING OF STORMWELL!
...UM.
HIGH FANTASY, HUH? THOUGHT YOU ONLY READ MYSTICAL-ARTS SCROLLS AND MEDICAL JOURNALS.
I REFUSE TO APOLOGIZE FOR READING ESCAPIST FICTION.
...THIS IS FICTION?
AH-HEM.

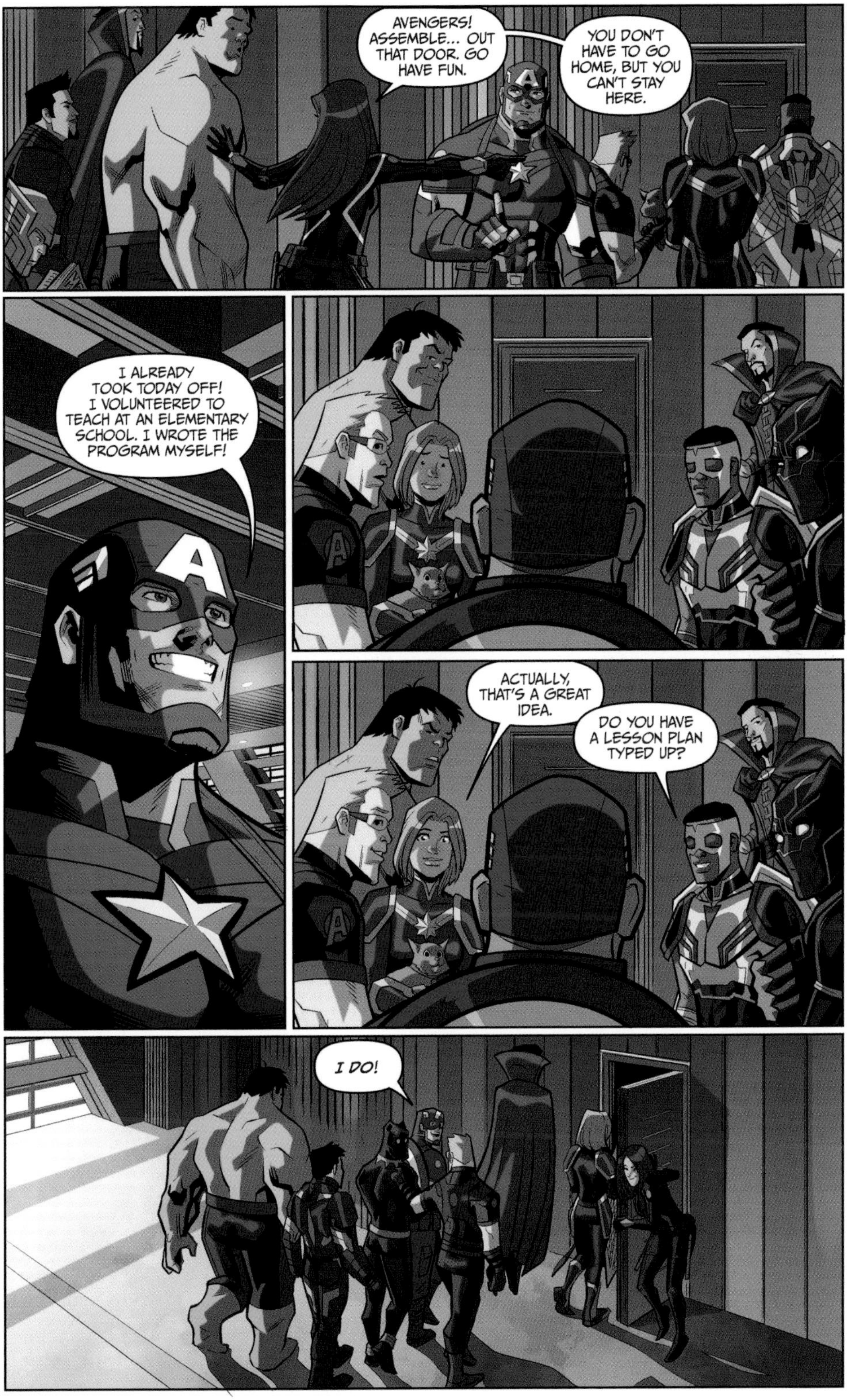
AVENGERS! ASSEMBLE... OUT THAT DOOR. GO HAVE FUN.
YOU DON'T HAVE TO GO HOME, BUT YOU CAN'T STAY HERE.
I ALREADY TOOK TODAY OFF! I VOLUNTEERED TO TEACH AT AN ELEMENTARY SCHOOL. I WROTE THE PROGRAM MYSELF!
ACTUALLY, THAT'S A GREAT IDEA.
DO YOU HAVE A LESSON PLAN TYPED UP?
I DO!

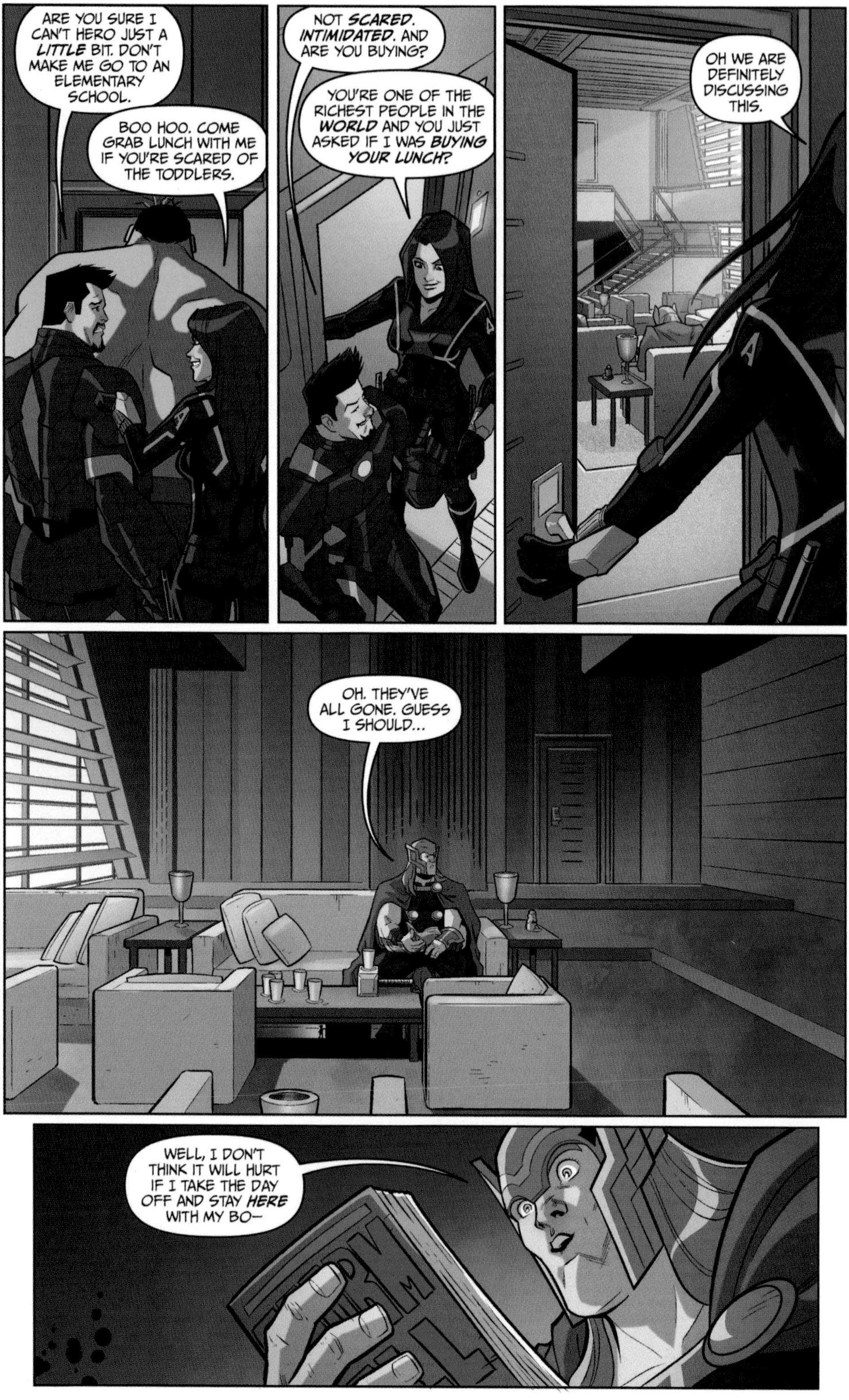

ARE YOU SURE I CAN'T HERO JUST A LITTLE BIT. DON'T MAKE ME GO TO AN ELEMENTARY SCHOOL.
BOO HOO. COME GRAB LUNCH WITH ME IF YOU'RE SCARED OF THE TODDLERS.
NOT SCARED. INTIMIDATED. AND ARE YOU BUYING?
YOU'RE ONE OF THE RICHEST PEOPLE IN THE WORLD AND YOU JUST ASKED IF I WAS BUYING YOUR LUNCH?
OH WE ARE DEFINITELY DISCUSSING THIS.
OH. THEY'VE ALL GONE. GUESS I SHOULD...
WELL, I DON'T THINK IT WILL HURT IF I TAKE THE DAY OFF AND STAY HERE WITH MY BO—

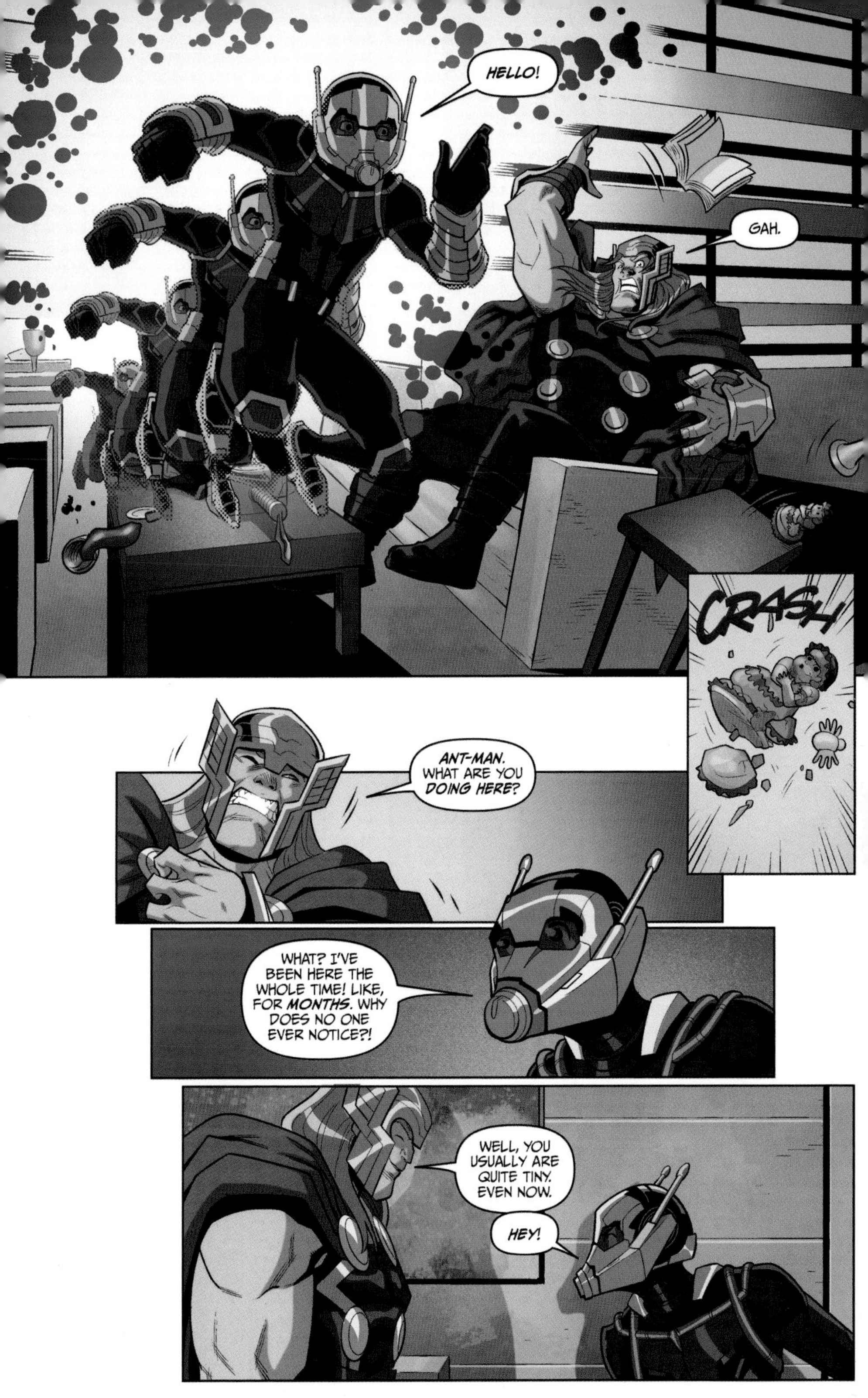
HELLO!
GAH.
CRASH
ANT-MAN. WHAT ARE YOU DOING HERE?
WHAT? I'VE BEEN HERE THE WHOLE TIME! LIKE, FOR MONTHS. WHY DOES NO ONE EVER NOTICE?!
WELL, YOU USUALLY ARE QUITE TINY. EVEN NOW.
HEY!

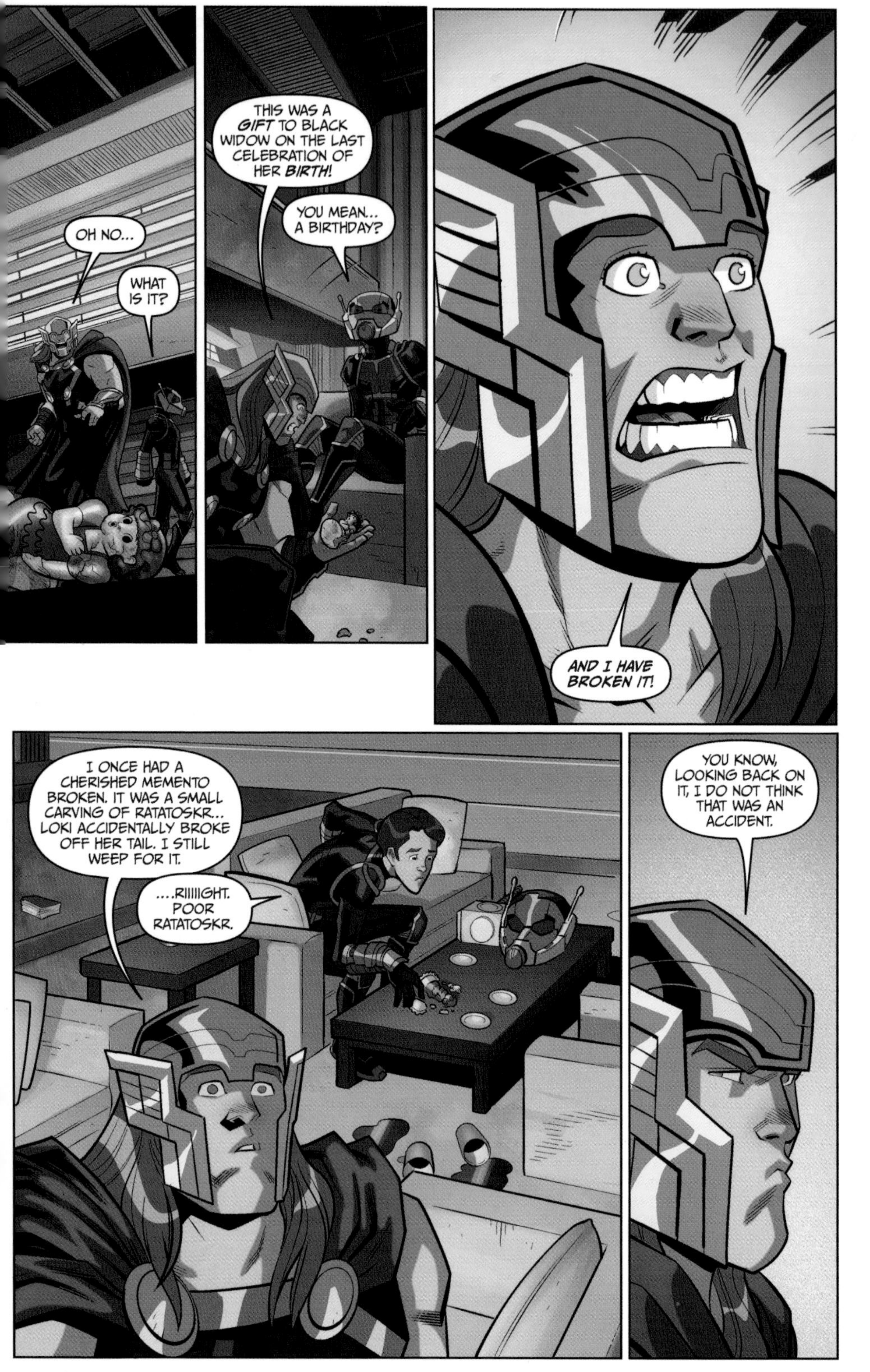

OH NO...
WHAT IS IT?
THIS WAS A *GIFT* TO BLACK WIDOW ON THE LAST CELEBRATION OF HER *BIRTH*!
YOU MEAN... A BIRTHDAY?
AND I HAVE BROKEN IT!
I ONCE HAD A CHERISHED MEMENTO BROKEN. IT WAS A SMALL CARVING OF RATATOSKR... LOKI ACCIDENTALLY BROKE OFF HER TAIL. I STILL WEEP FOR IT.
....RIIIIIGHT. POOR RATATOSKR.
YOU KNOW, LOOKING BACK ON IT, I DO NOT THINK THAT WAS AN ACCIDENT.

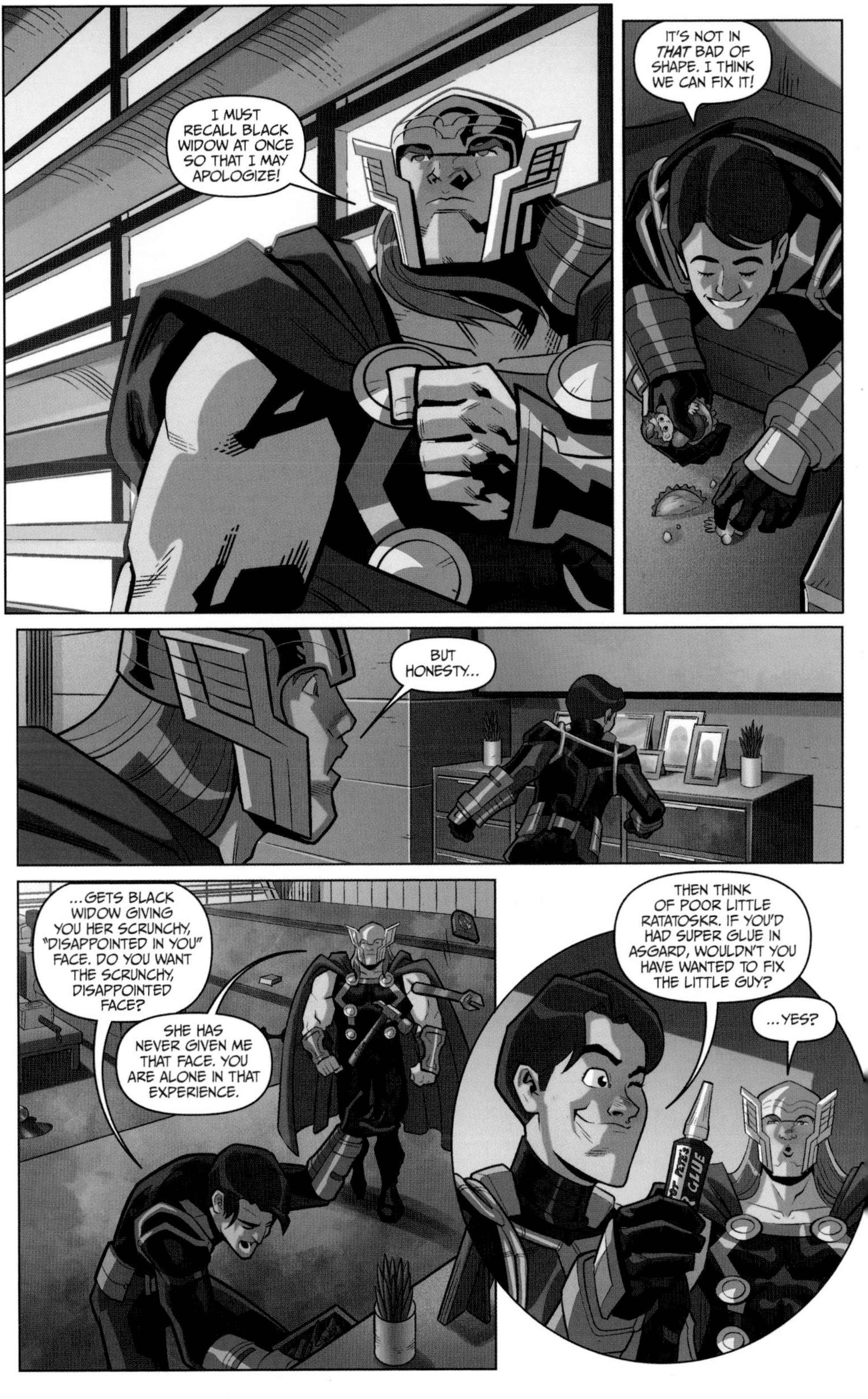
I MUST RECALL BLACK WIDOW AT ONCE SO THAT I MAY APOLOGIZE!
IT'S NOT IN *THAT* BAD OF SHAPE. I THINK WE CAN FIX IT!
BUT HONESTY...
...GETS BLACK WIDOW GIVING YOU HER SCRUNCHY, "DISAPPOINTED IN YOU" FACE. DO YOU WANT THE SCRUNCHY, DISAPPOINTED FACE?
SHE HAS NEVER GIVEN ME THAT FACE. YOU ARE ALONE IN THAT EXPERIENCE.
THEN THINK OF POOR LITTLE RATATOSKR. IF YOU'D HAD SUPER GLUE IN ASGARD, WOULDN'T YOU HAVE WANTED TO FIX THE LITTLE GUY?
...YES?

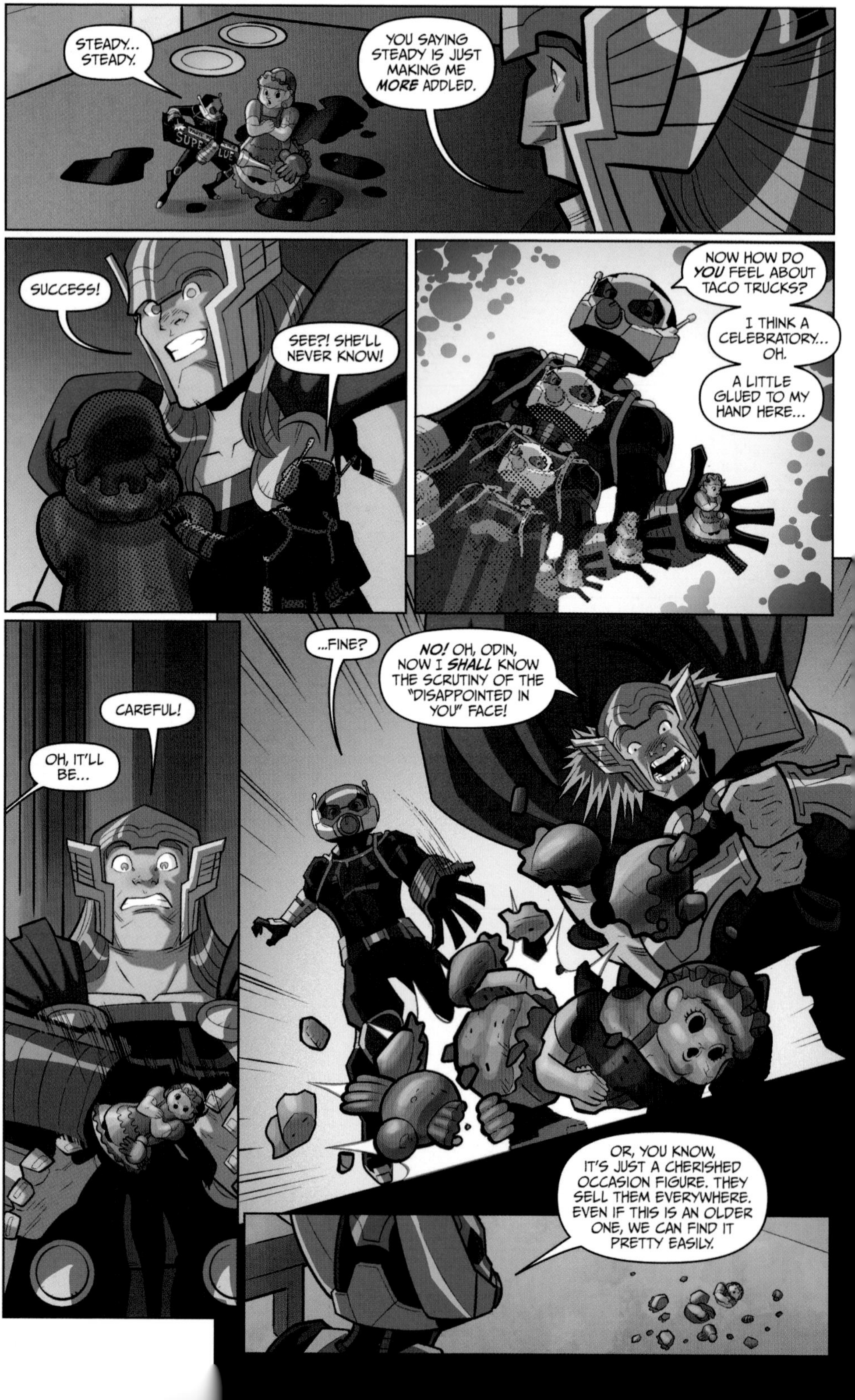
STEADY... STEADY.
YOU SAYING STEADY IS JUST MAKING ME *MORE* ADDLED.
SUPER GLUE
SUCCESS!
SEE?! SHE'LL NEVER KNOW!
NOW HOW DO *YOU* FEEL ABOUT TACO TRUCKS?
I THINK A CELEBRATORY... OH.
A LITTLE GLUED TO MY HAND HERE...
OH, IT'LL BE...
CAREFUL!
...FINE?
NO! OH, ODIN, NOW I *SHALL* KNOW THE SCRUTINY OF THE "DISAPPOINTED IN YOU" FACE!
OR, YOU KNOW, IT'S JUST A CHERISHED OCCASION FIGURE. THEY SELL THEM EVERYWHERE. EVEN IF THIS IS AN OLDER ONE, WE CAN FIND IT PRETTY EASILY.

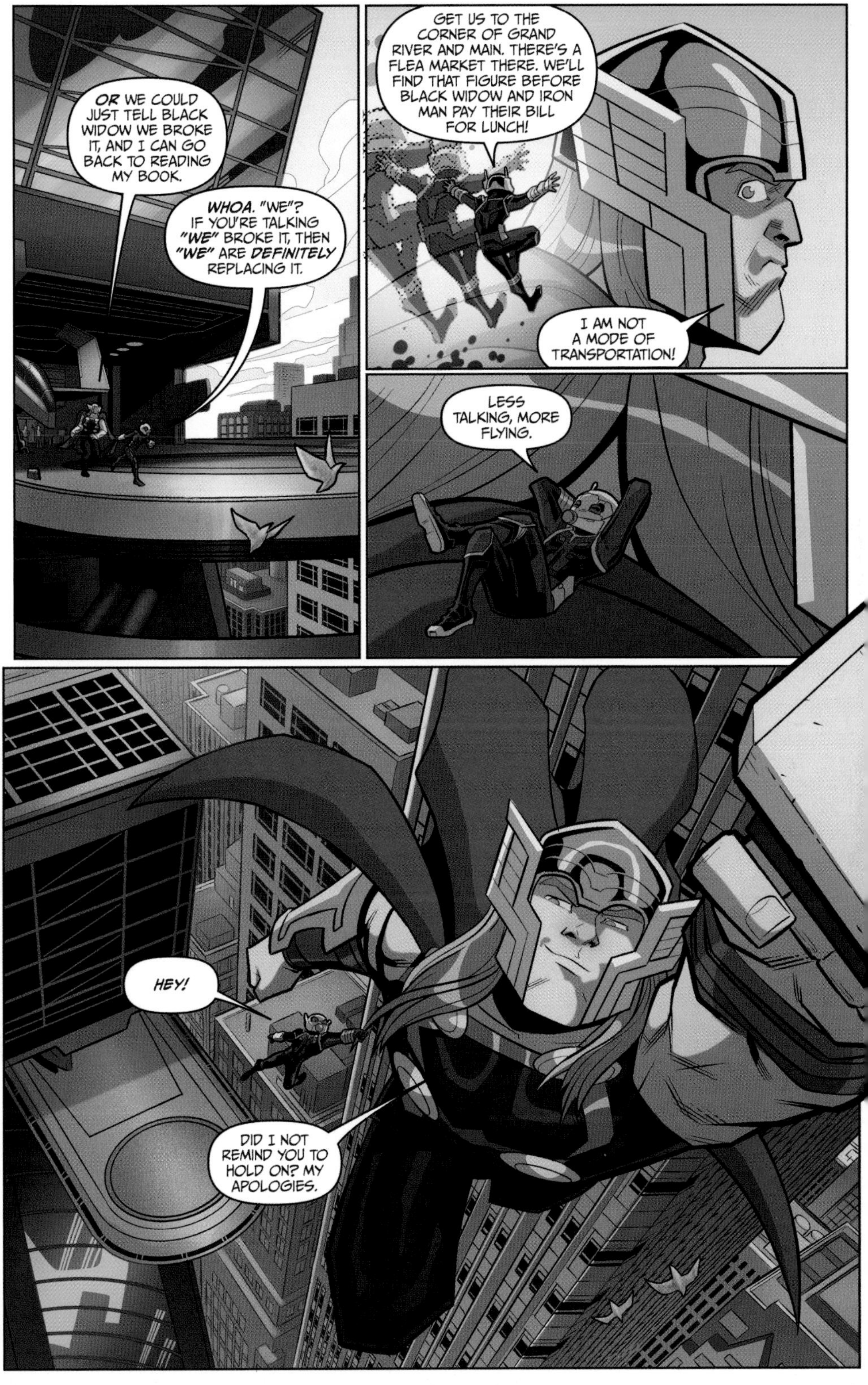

OR WE COULD JUST TELL BLACK WIDOW WE BROKE IT, AND I CAN GO BACK TO READING MY BOOK.
WHOA. "WE"? IF YOU'RE TALKING "WE" BROKE IT, THEN "WE" ARE DEFINITELY REPLACING IT.
GET US TO THE CORNER OF GRAND RIVER AND MAIN. THERE'S A FLEA MARKET THERE. WE'LL FIND THAT FIGURE BEFORE BLACK WIDOW AND IRON MAN PAY THEIR BILL FOR LUNCH!
I AM NOT A MODE OF TRANSPORTATION!
LESS TALKING, MORE FLYING.
HEY!
DID I NOT REMIND YOU TO HOLD ON? MY APOLOGIES.

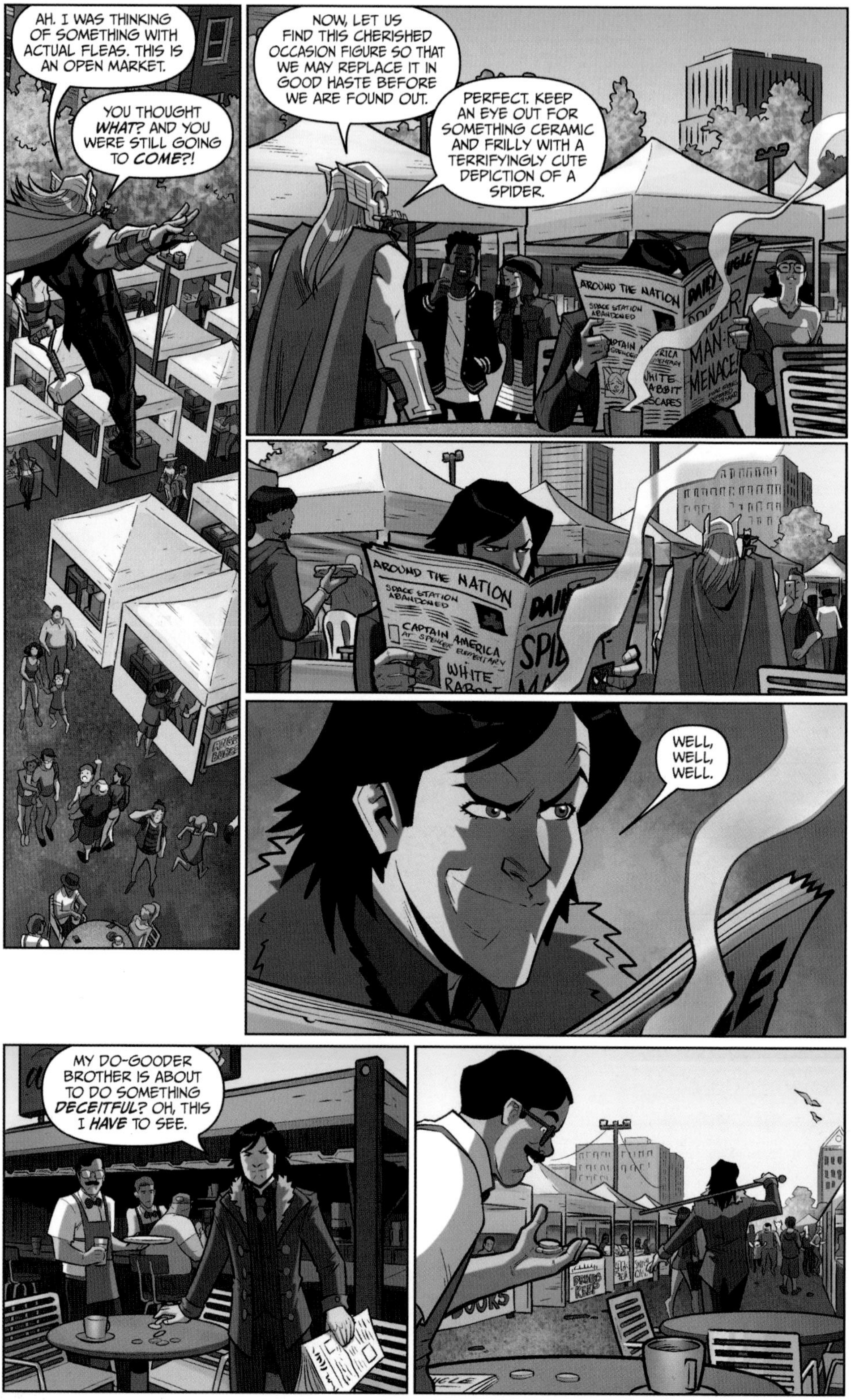
AH. I WAS THINKING OF SOMETHING WITH ACTUAL FLEAS. THIS IS AN OPEN MARKET.
YOU THOUGHT *WHAT?* AND YOU WERE STILL GOING TO *COME?!*
NOW, LET US FIND THIS CHERISHED OCCASION FIGURE SO THAT WE MAY REPLACE IT IN GOOD HASTE BEFORE WE ARE FOUND OUT.
PERFECT. KEEP AN EYE OUT FOR SOMETHING CERAMIC AND FRILLY WITH A TERRIFYINGLY CUTE DEPICTION OF A SPIDER.
AROUND THE NATION
SPACE STATION ABANDONED
CAPTAIN AMERICA AT SPENCER ELEMENTARY
WHITE RABBIT ESCAPES
SPIDER-MAN-MENACE!
WELL, WELL, WELL.
MY DO-GOODER BROTHER IS ABOUT TO DO SOMETHING *DECEITFUL?* OH, THIS I *HAVE* TO SEE.

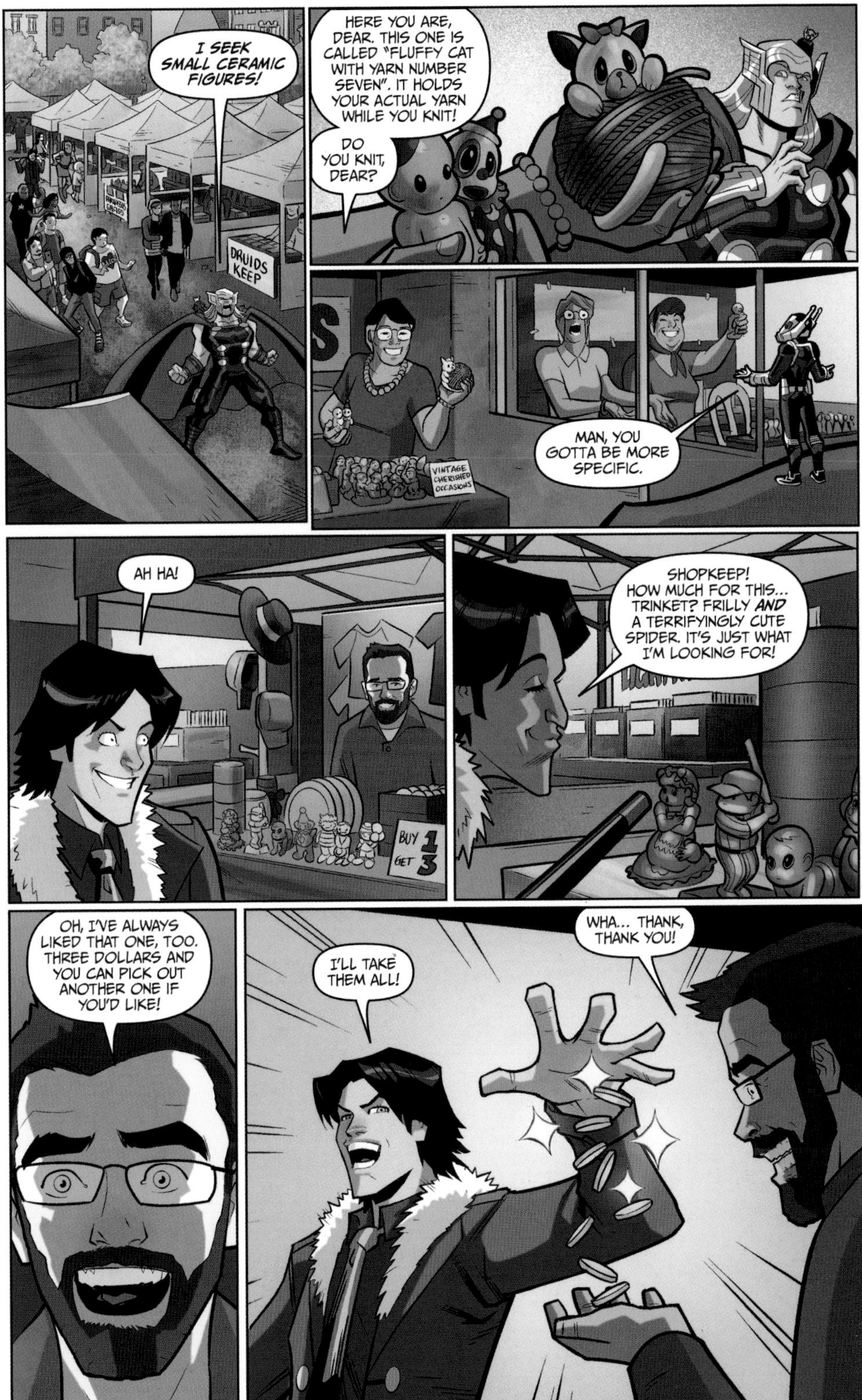
I SEEK SMALL CERAMIC FIGURES!
DRUIDS KEEP
HERE YOU ARE, DEAR. THIS ONE IS CALLED "FLUFFY CAT WITH YARN NUMBER SEVEN". IT HOLDS YOUR ACTUAL YARN WHILE YOU KNIT!
DO YOU KNIT, DEAR?
VINTAGE CHERISHED OCCASIONS
MAN, YOU GOTTA BE MORE SPECIFIC.
AH HA!
BUY 1 GET 3
SHOPKEEP! HOW MUCH FOR THIS... TRINKET? FRILLY AND A TERRIFYINGLY CUTE SPIDER. IT'S JUST WHAT I'M LOOKING FOR!
OH, I'VE ALWAYS LIKED THAT ONE, TOO. THREE DOLLARS AND YOU CAN PICK OUT ANOTHER ONE IF YOU'D LIKE!
I'LL TAKE THEM ALL!
WHA... THANK, THANK YOU!

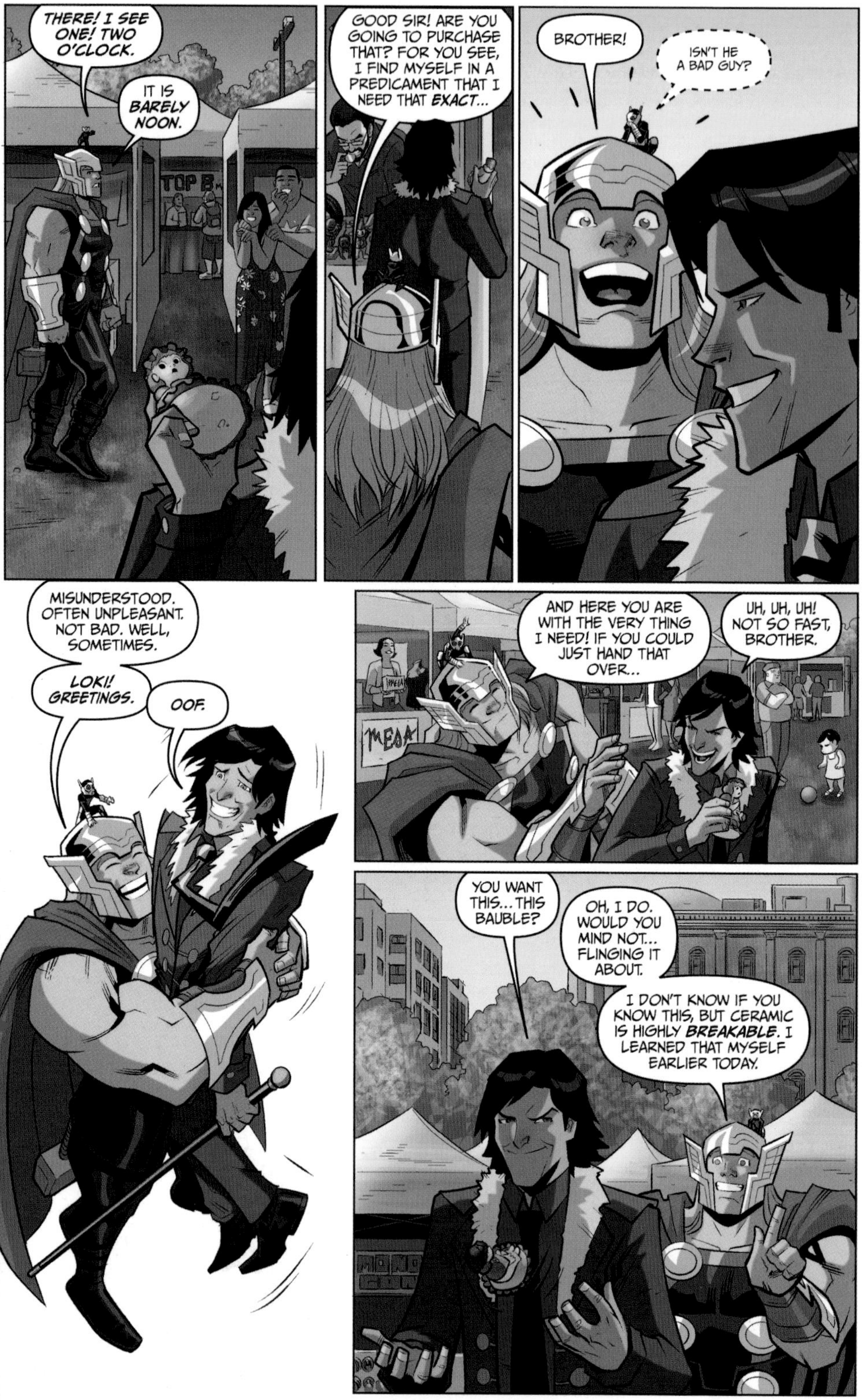
THERE! I SEE ONE! TWO O'CLOCK.
IT IS BARELY NOON.
TOP B
GOOD SIR! ARE YOU GOING TO PURCHASE THAT? FOR YOU SEE, I FIND MYSELF IN A PREDICAMENT THAT I NEED THAT EXACT...
BROTHER!
ISN'T HE A BAD GUY?
MISUNDERSTOOD. OFTEN UNPLEASANT. NOT BAD. WELL, SOMETIMES.
LOKI! GREETINGS.
OOF.
AND HERE YOU ARE WITH THE VERY THING I NEED! IF YOU COULD JUST HAND THAT OVER...
UH, UH, UH! NOT SO FAST, BROTHER.
MESA
YOU WANT THIS... THIS BAUBLE?
OH, I DO. WOULD YOU MIND NOT... FLINGING IT ABOUT.
I DON'T KNOW IF YOU KNOW THIS, BUT CERAMIC IS HIGHLY BREAKABLE. I LEARNED THAT MYSELF EARLIER TODAY.

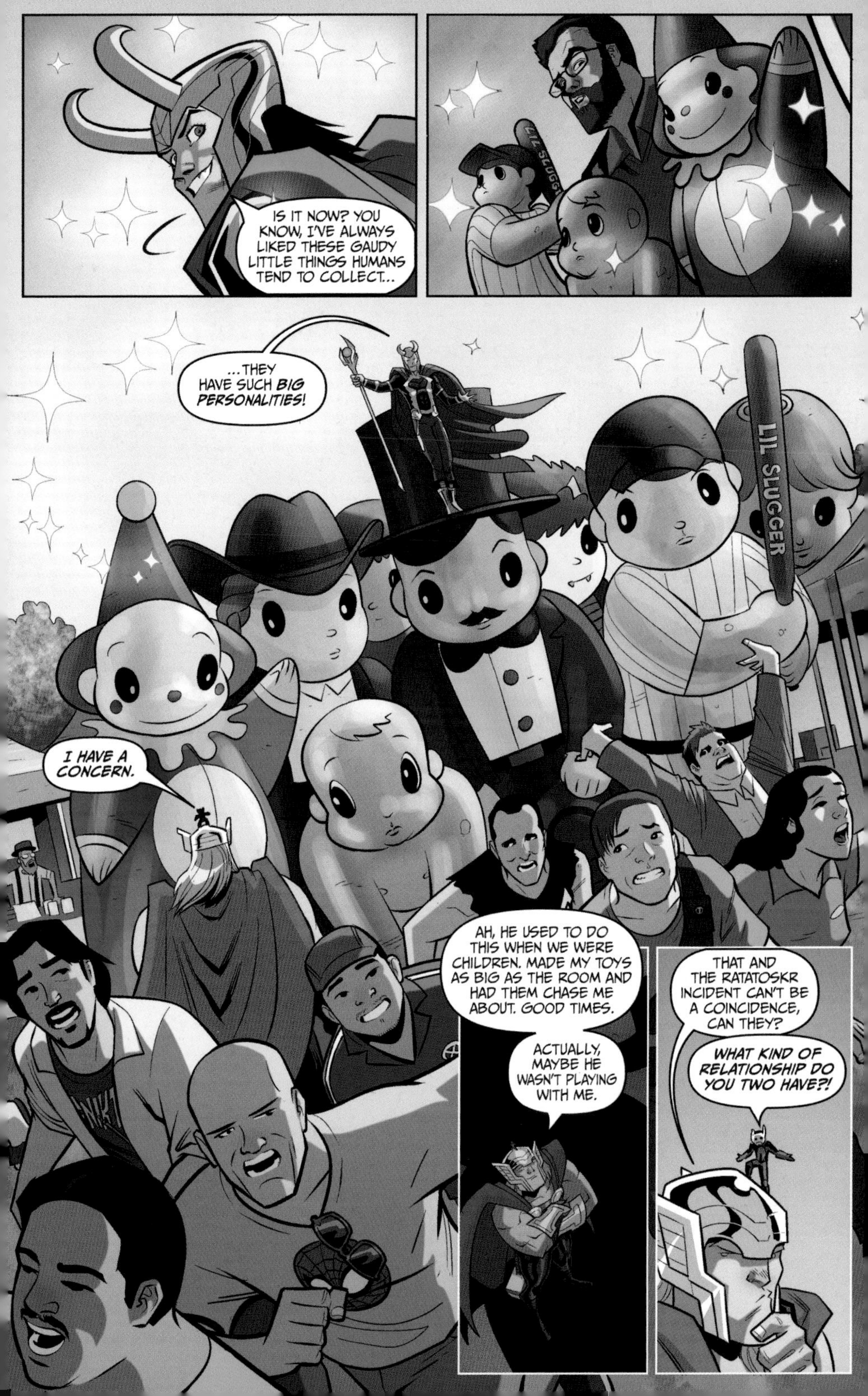
IS IT NOW? YOU KNOW, I'VE ALWAYS LIKED THESE GAUDY LITTLE THINGS HUMANS TEND TO COLLECT...
LI'L SLUGGER
...THEY HAVE SUCH BIG PERSONALITIES!
LI'L SLUGGER
I HAVE A CONCERN.
AH, HE USED TO DO THIS WHEN WE WERE CHILDREN. MADE MY TOYS AS BIG AS THE ROOM AND HAD THEM CHASE ME ABOUT. GOOD TIMES.
ACTUALLY, MAYBE HE WASN'T PLAYING WITH ME.
THAT AND THE RATATOSKR INCIDENT CAN'T BE A COINCIDENCE, CAN THEY?
WHAT KIND OF RELATIONSHIP DO YOU TWO HAVE?!

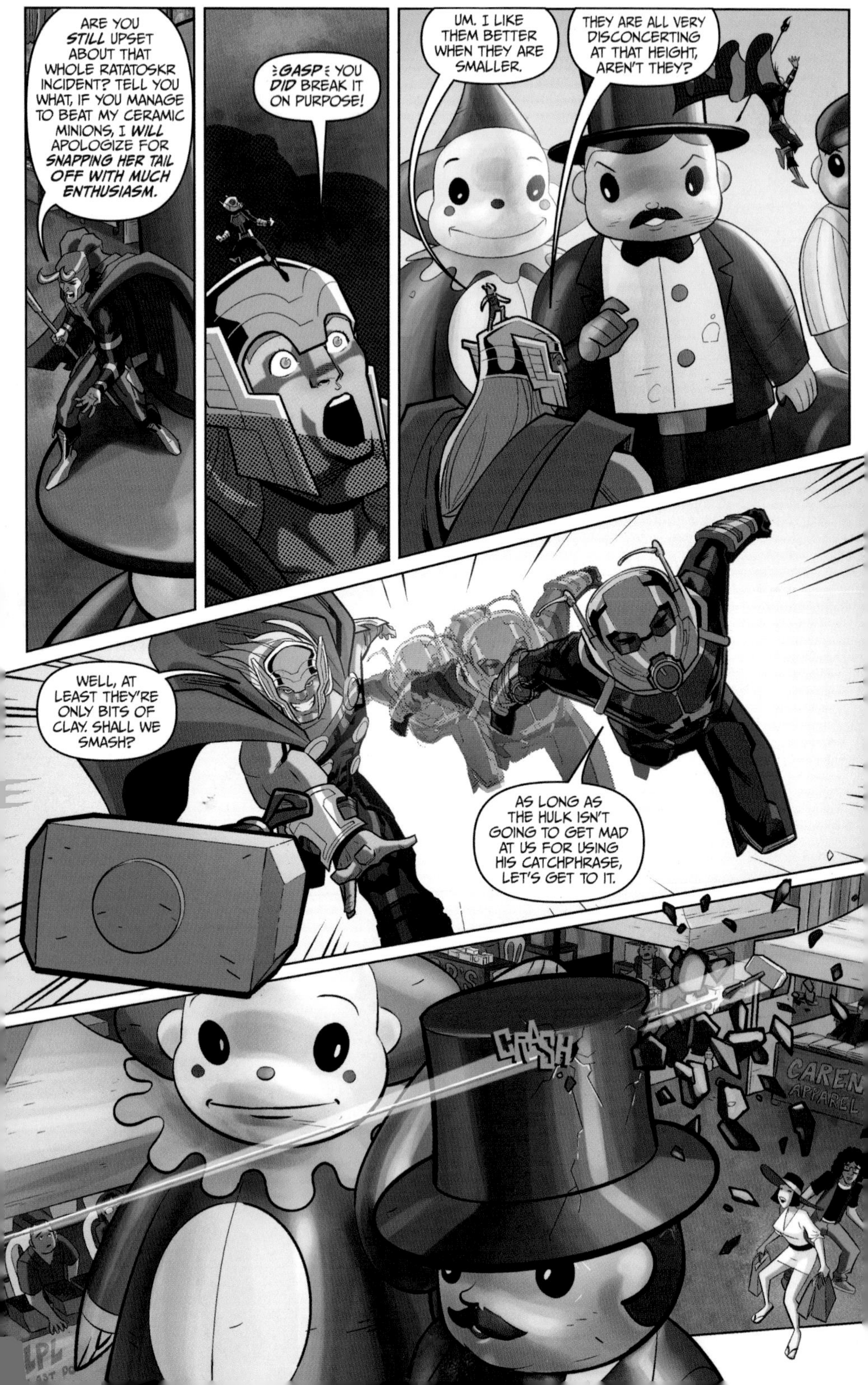
ARE YOU STILL UPSET ABOUT THAT WHOLE RATATOSKR INCIDENT? TELL YOU WHAT, IF YOU MANAGE TO BEAT MY CERAMIC MINIONS, I WILL APOLOGIZE FOR SNAPPING HER TAIL OFF WITH MUCH ENTHUSIASM.
GASP YOU DID BREAK IT ON PURPOSE!
UM. I LIKE THEM BETTER WHEN THEY ARE SMALLER.
THEY ARE ALL VERY DISCONCERTING AT THAT HEIGHT, AREN'T THEY?
WELL, AT LEAST THEY'RE ONLY BITS OF CLAY. SHALL WE SMASH?
AS LONG AS THE HULK ISN'T GOING TO GET MAD AT US FOR USING HIS CATCHPHRASE, LET'S GET TO IT.
CRASH!
CAREN APPAREL

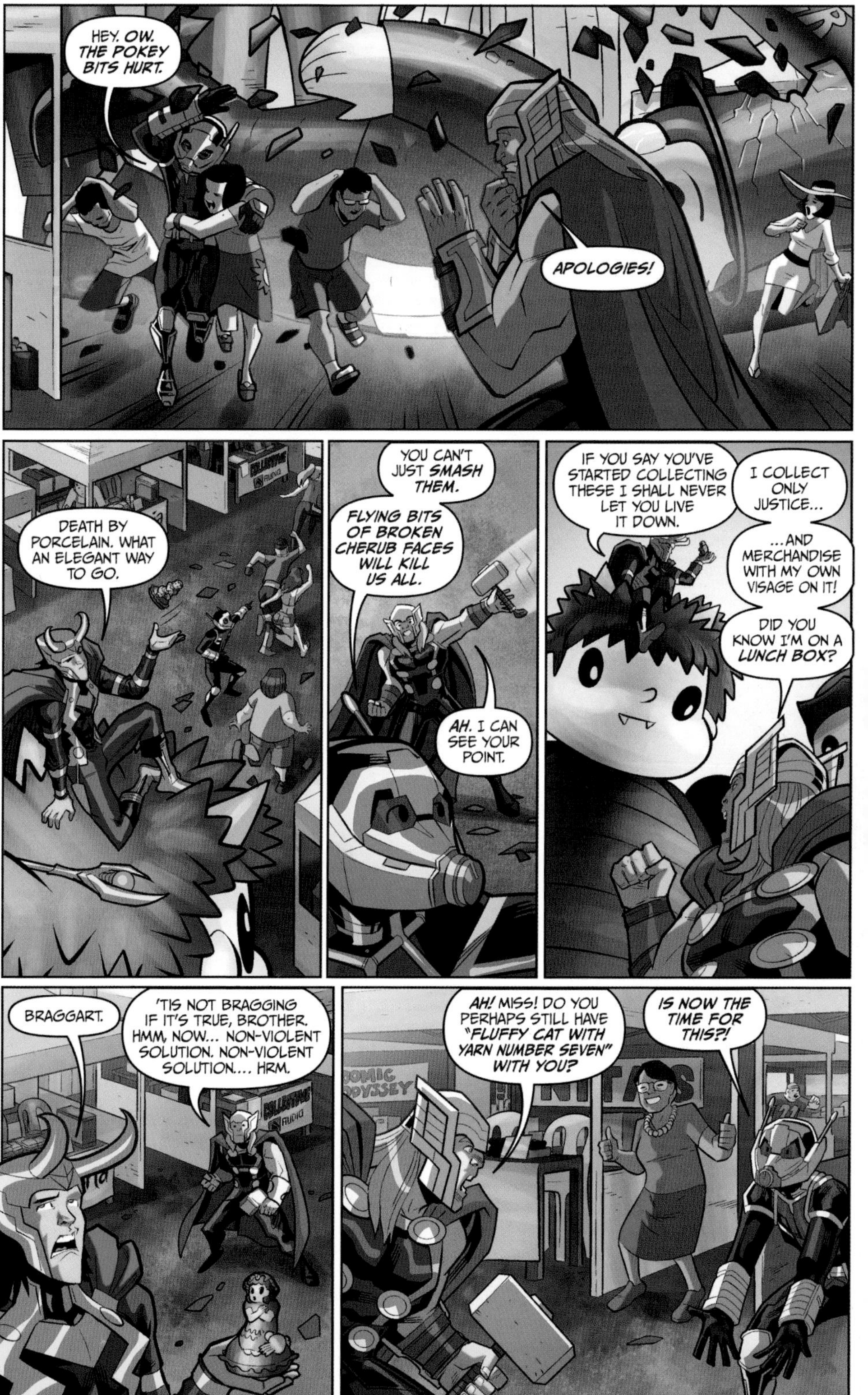
HEY. OW. THE POKEY BITS HURT.
APOLOGIES!
DEATH BY PORCELAIN. WHAT AN ELEGANT WAY TO GO.
YOU CAN'T JUST SMASH THEM.
FLYING BITS OF BROKEN CHERUB FACES WILL KILL US ALL.
AH. I CAN SEE YOUR POINT.
IF YOU SAY YOU'VE STARTED COLLECTING THESE I SHALL NEVER LET YOU LIVE IT DOWN.
I COLLECT ONLY JUSTICE...
...AND MERCHANDISE WITH MY OWN VISAGE ON IT!
DID YOU KNOW I'M ON A LUNCH BOX?
BRAGGART.
'TIS NOT BRAGGING IF IT'S TRUE, BROTHER. HMM, NOW... NON-VIOLENT SOLUTION. NON-VIOLENT SOLUTION.... HRM.
AH! MISS! DO YOU PERHAPS STILL HAVE "FLUFFY CAT WITH YARN NUMBER SEVEN" WITH YOU?
IS NOW THE TIME FOR THIS?!

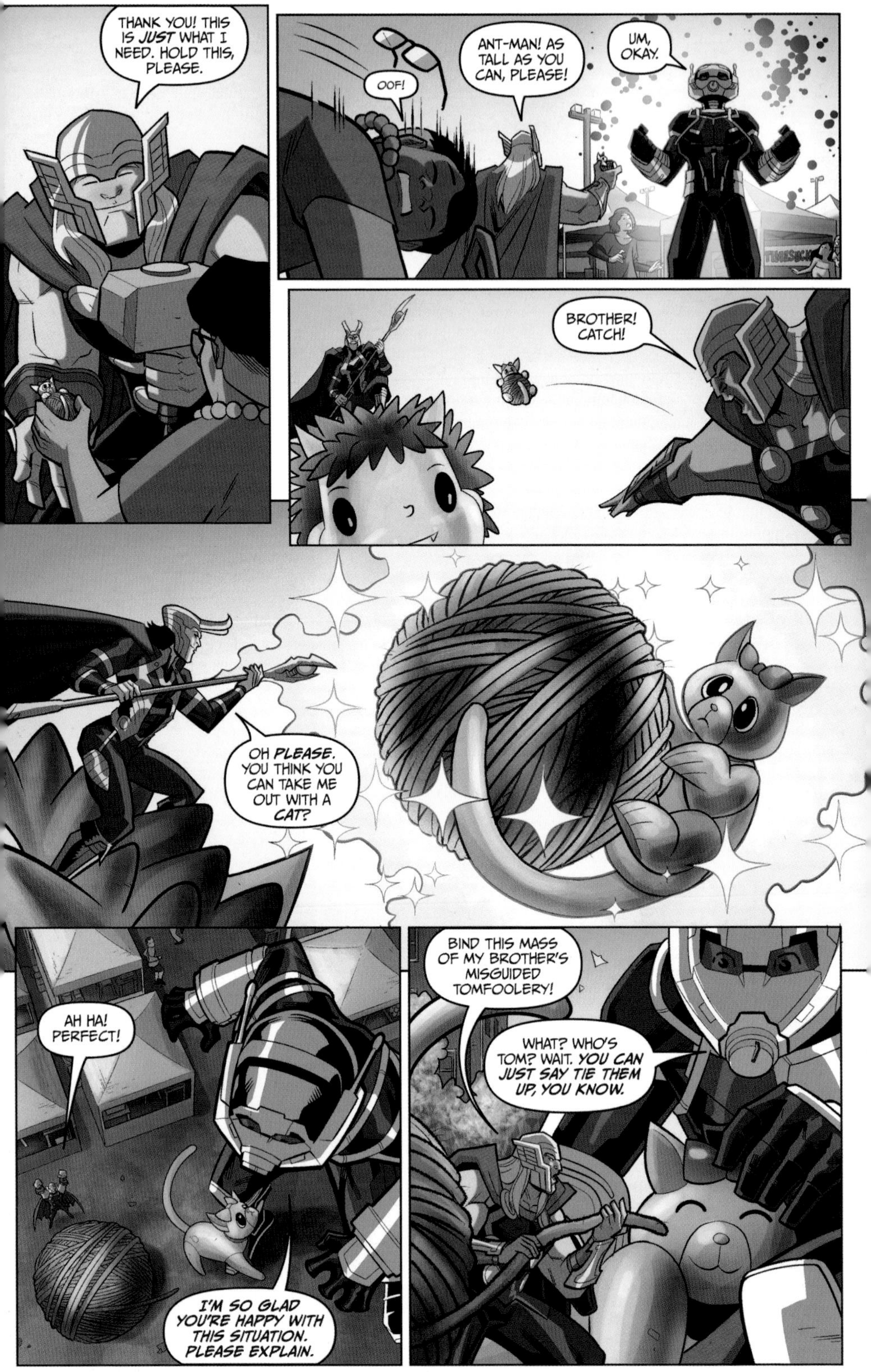
THANK YOU! THIS IS *JUST* WHAT I NEED. HOLD THIS, PLEASE.
OOF!
ANT-MAN! AS TALL AS YOU CAN, PLEASE!
UM, OKAY.
BROTHER! CATCH!
OH *PLEASE*. YOU THINK YOU CAN TAKE ME OUT WITH A *CAT*?
AH HA! PERFECT!
I'M SO GLAD YOU'RE HAPPY WITH THIS SITUATION. PLEASE EXPLAIN.
BIND THIS MASS OF MY BROTHER'S MISGUIDED TOMFOOLERY!
WHAT? WHO'S TOM? WAIT. *YOU CAN JUST SAY TIE THEM UP, YOU KNOW.*

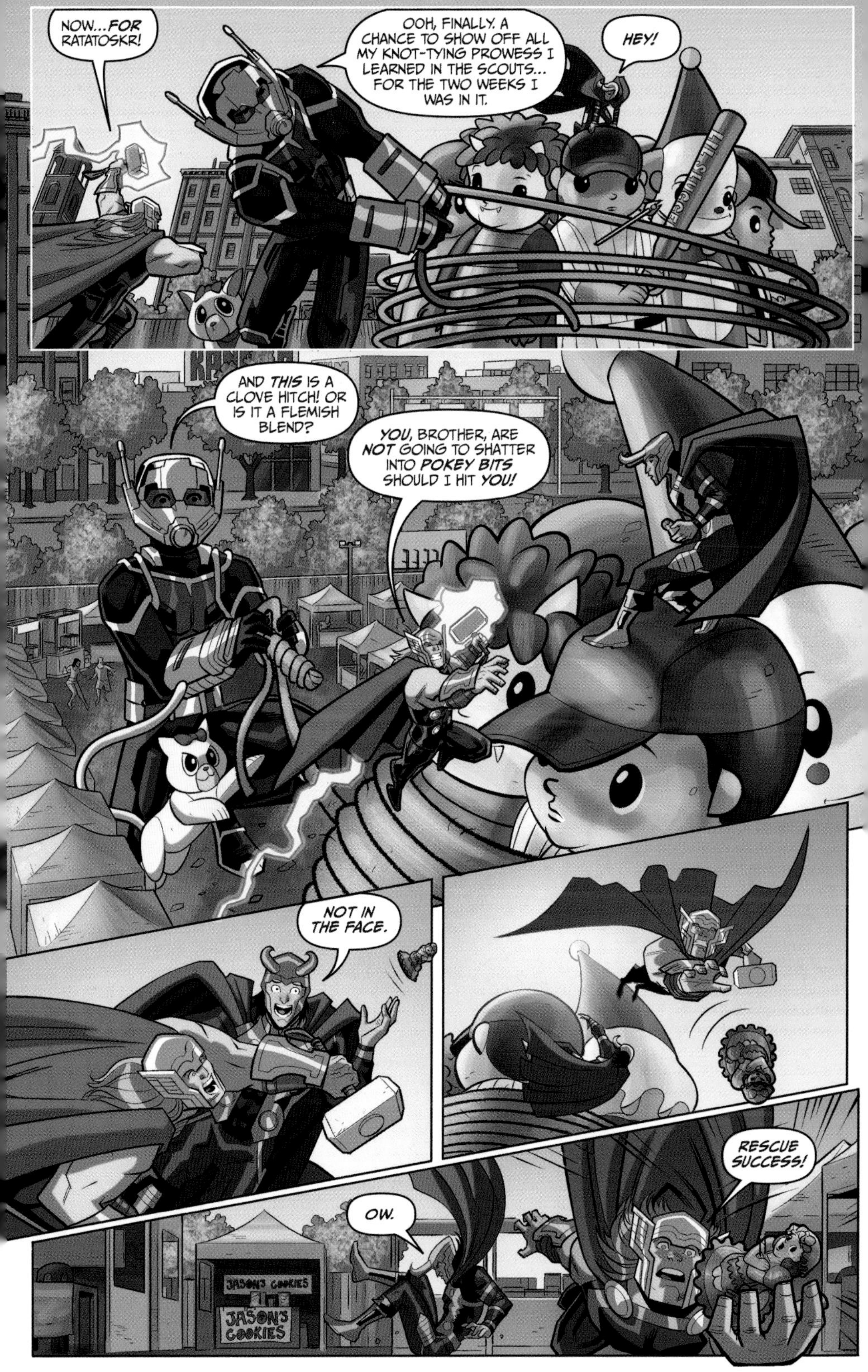
NOW...FOR RATATOSKR!
OOH, FINALLY. A CHANCE TO SHOW OFF ALL MY KNOT-TYING PROWESS I LEARNED IN THE SCOUTS... FOR THE TWO WEEKS I WAS IN IT.
HEY!
LIL SLUGGER
AND THIS IS A CLOVE HITCH! OR IS IT A FLEMISH BLEND?
YOU, BROTHER, ARE NOT GOING TO SHATTER INTO POKEY BITS SHOULD I HIT YOU!
NOT IN THE FACE.
RESCUE SUCCESS!
OW.
JASON'S COOKIES
JASON'S COOKIES

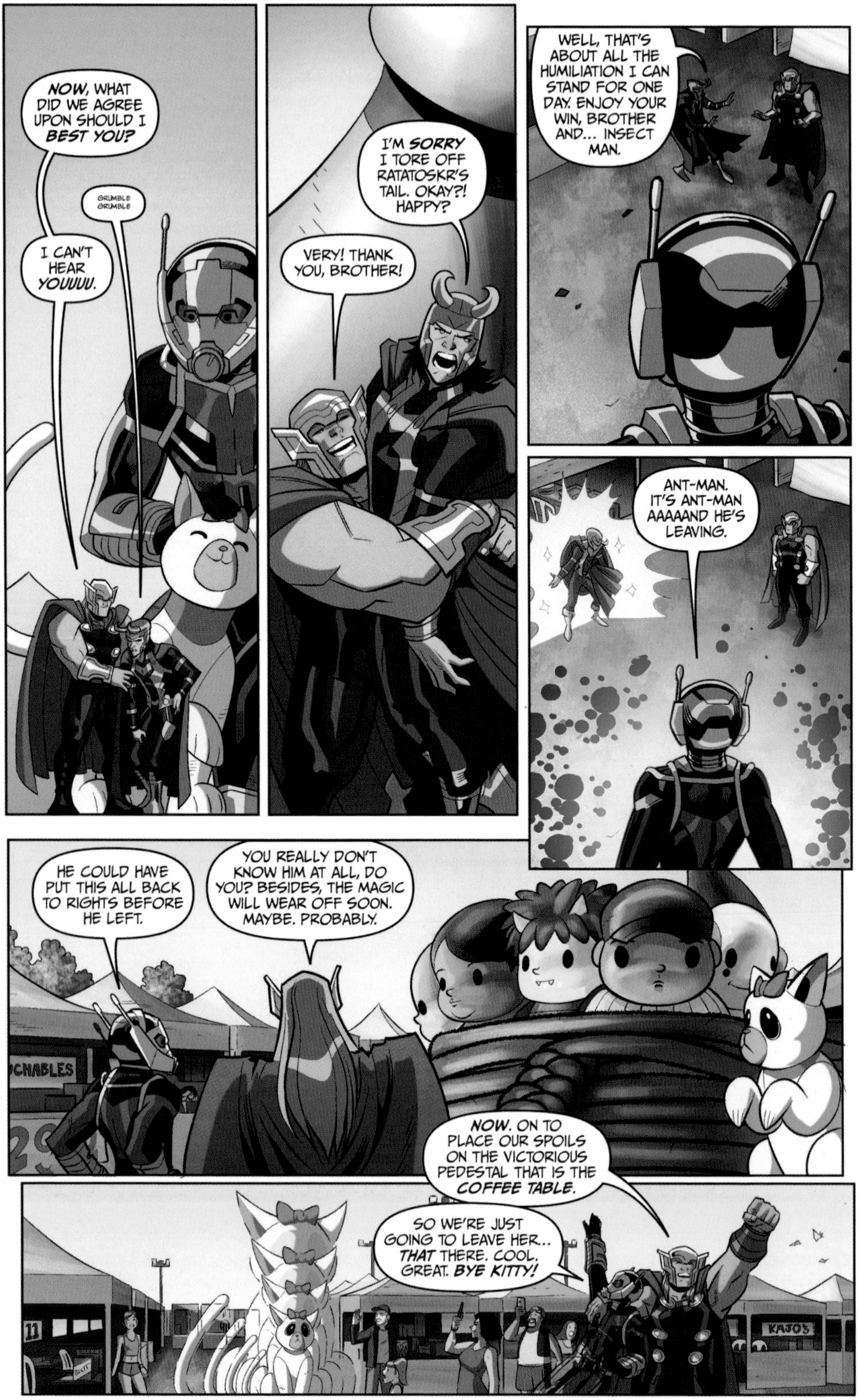
NOW, WHAT DID WE AGREE UPON SHOULD I BEST YOU?
GRUMBLE GRUMBLE
I CAN'T HEAR YOUUUU.
I'M SORRY I TORE OFF RATATOSKR'S TAIL. OKAY?! HAPPY?
VERY! THANK YOU, BROTHER!
WELL, THAT'S ABOUT ALL THE HUMILIATION I CAN STAND FOR ONE DAY. ENJOY YOUR WIN, BROTHER AND... INSECT MAN.
ANT-MAN. IT'S ANT-MAN AAAAAND HE'S LEAVING.
HE COULD HAVE PUT THIS ALL BACK TO RIGHTS BEFORE HE LEFT.
YOU REALLY DON'T KNOW HIM AT ALL, DO YOU? BESIDES, THE MAGIC WILL WEAR OFF SOON. MAYBE. PROBABLY.
UCHABLES
NOW. ON TO PLACE OUR SPOILS ON THE VICTORIOUS PEDESTAL THAT IS THE COFFEE TABLE.
SO WE'RE JUST GOING TO LEAVE HER... THAT THERE. COOL. GREAT. BYE KITTY!
KAJO'S

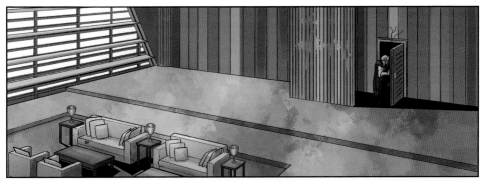

THOR?

GAH.

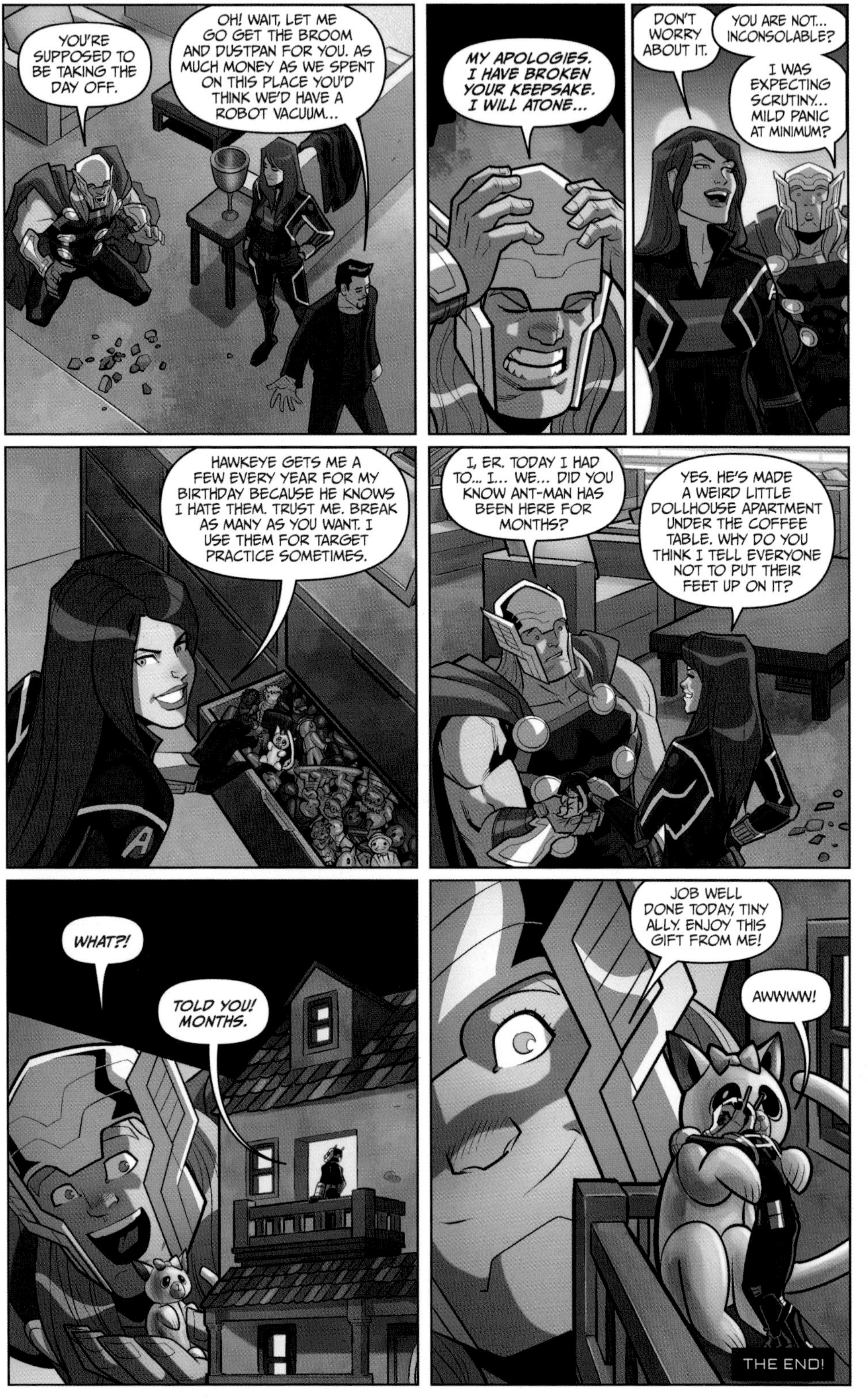
YOU'RE SUPPOSED TO BE TAKING THE DAY OFF.
OH! WAIT, LET ME GO GET THE BROOM AND DUSTPAN FOR YOU. AS MUCH MONEY AS WE SPENT ON THIS PLACE YOU'D THINK WE'D HAVE A ROBOT VACUUM...
MY APOLOGIES. I HAVE BROKEN YOUR KEEPSAKE. I WILL ATONE...
DON'T WORRY ABOUT IT.
YOU ARE NOT... INCONSOLABLE?
I WAS EXPECTING SCRUTINY... MILD PANIC AT MINIMUM?
HAWKEYE GETS ME A FEW EVERY YEAR FOR MY BIRTHDAY BECAUSE HE KNOWS I HATE THEM. TRUST ME. BREAK AS MANY AS YOU WANT. I USE THEM FOR TARGET PRACTICE SOMETIMES.
I, ER. TODAY I HAD TO... I... WE... DID YOU KNOW ANT-MAN HAS BEEN HERE FOR MONTHS?
YES. HE'S MADE A WEIRD LITTLE DOLLHOUSE APARTMENT UNDER THE COFFEE TABLE. WHY DO YOU THINK I TELL EVERYONE NOT TO PUT THEIR FEET UP ON IT?
WHAT?!
TOLD YOU! MONTHS.
JOB WELL DONE TODAY, TINY ALLY. ENJOY THIS GIFT FROM ME!
AWWWW!
THE END!

ART BY: JACOB EDGAR
COLORS BY: PROTOBUNKER

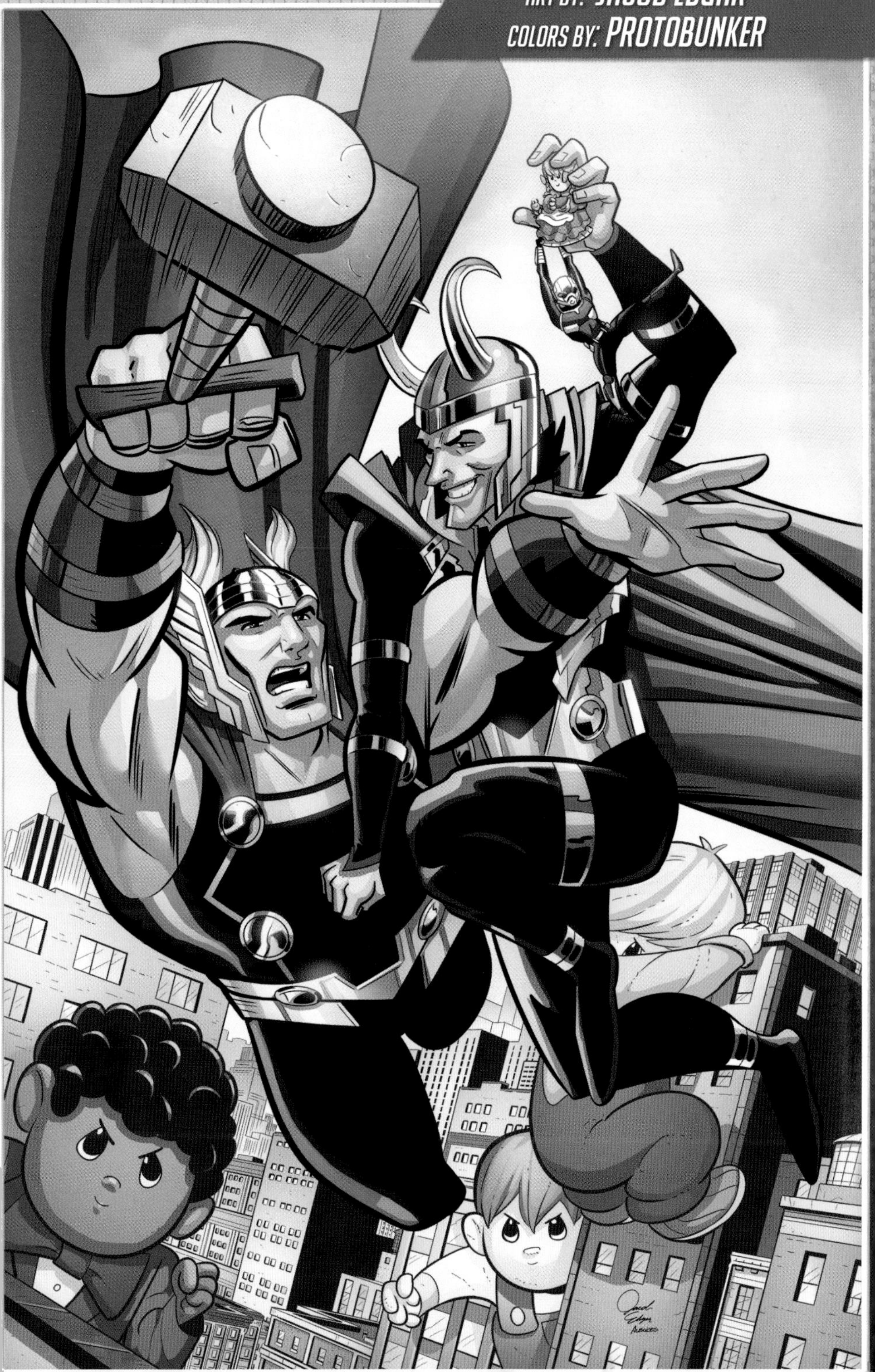

ART BY: BUTCH MAPA

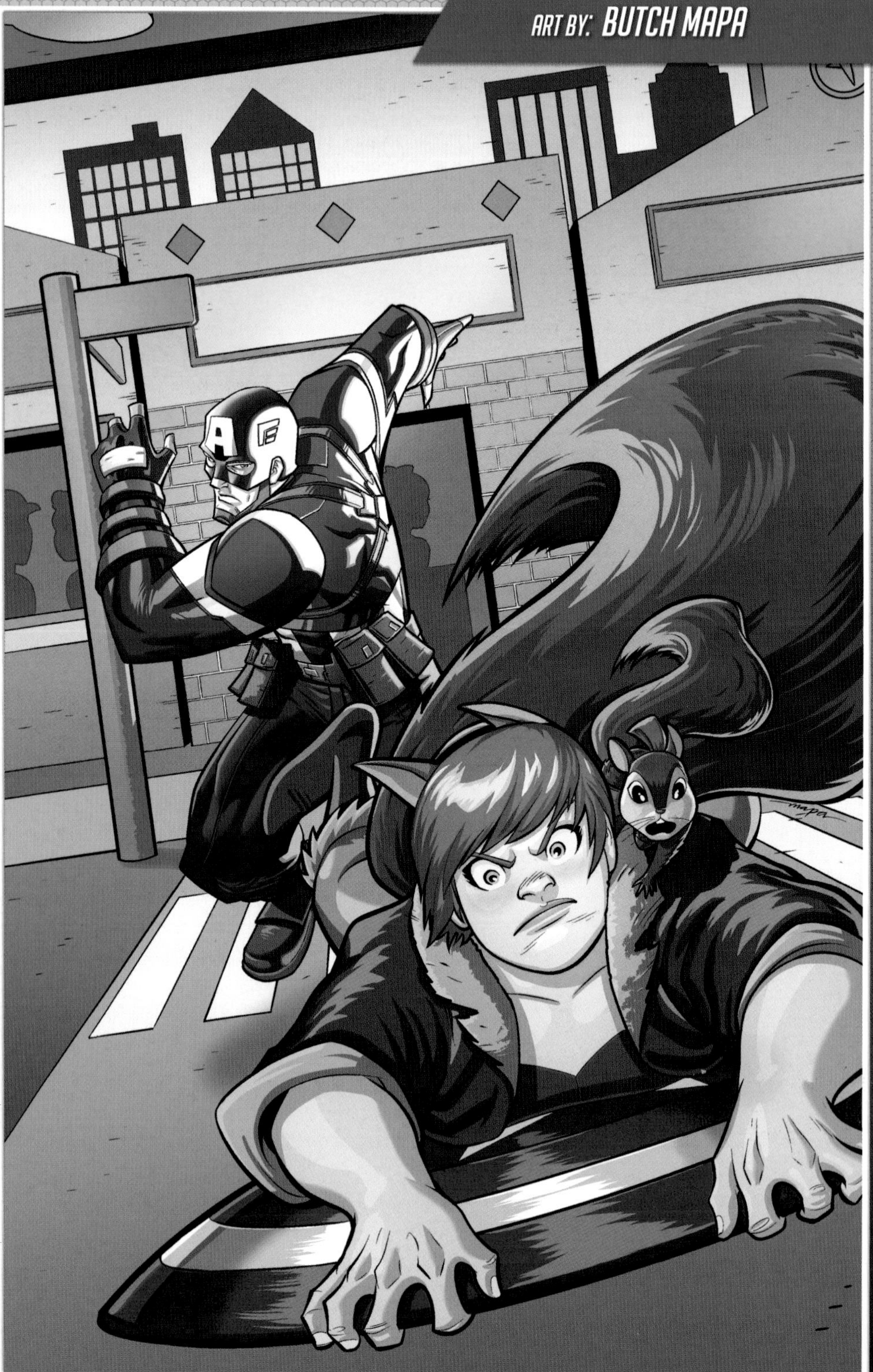
mapa

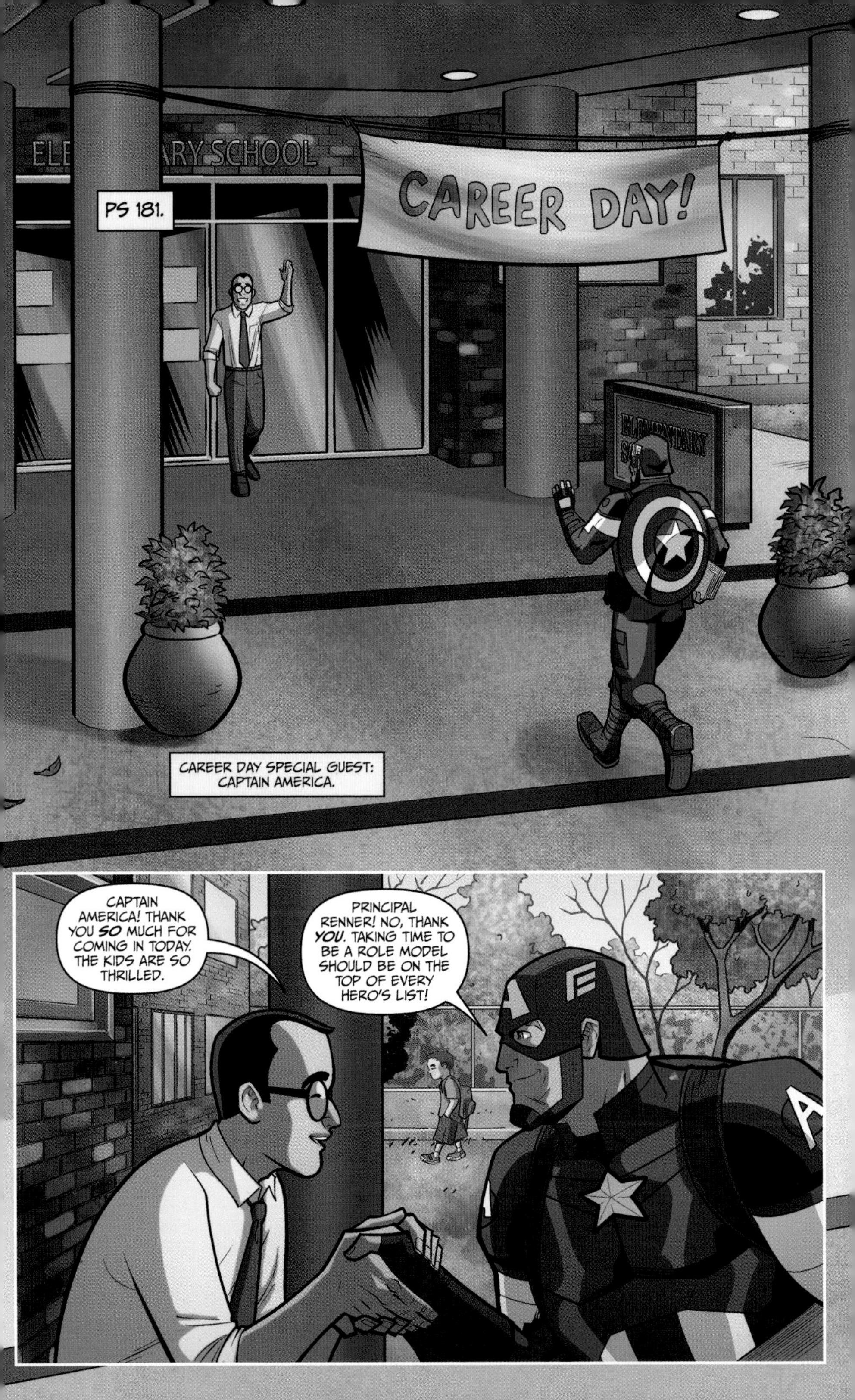
PS 181.
CAREER DAY!
CAREER DAY SPECIAL GUEST: CAPTAIN AMERICA.
CAPTAIN AMERICA! THANK YOU **SO** MUCH FOR COMING IN TODAY. THE KIDS ARE SO THRILLED.
PRINCIPAL RENNER! NO, THANK **YOU**. TAKING TIME TO BE A ROLE MODEL SHOULD BE ON THE TOP OF EVERY HERO'S LIST!

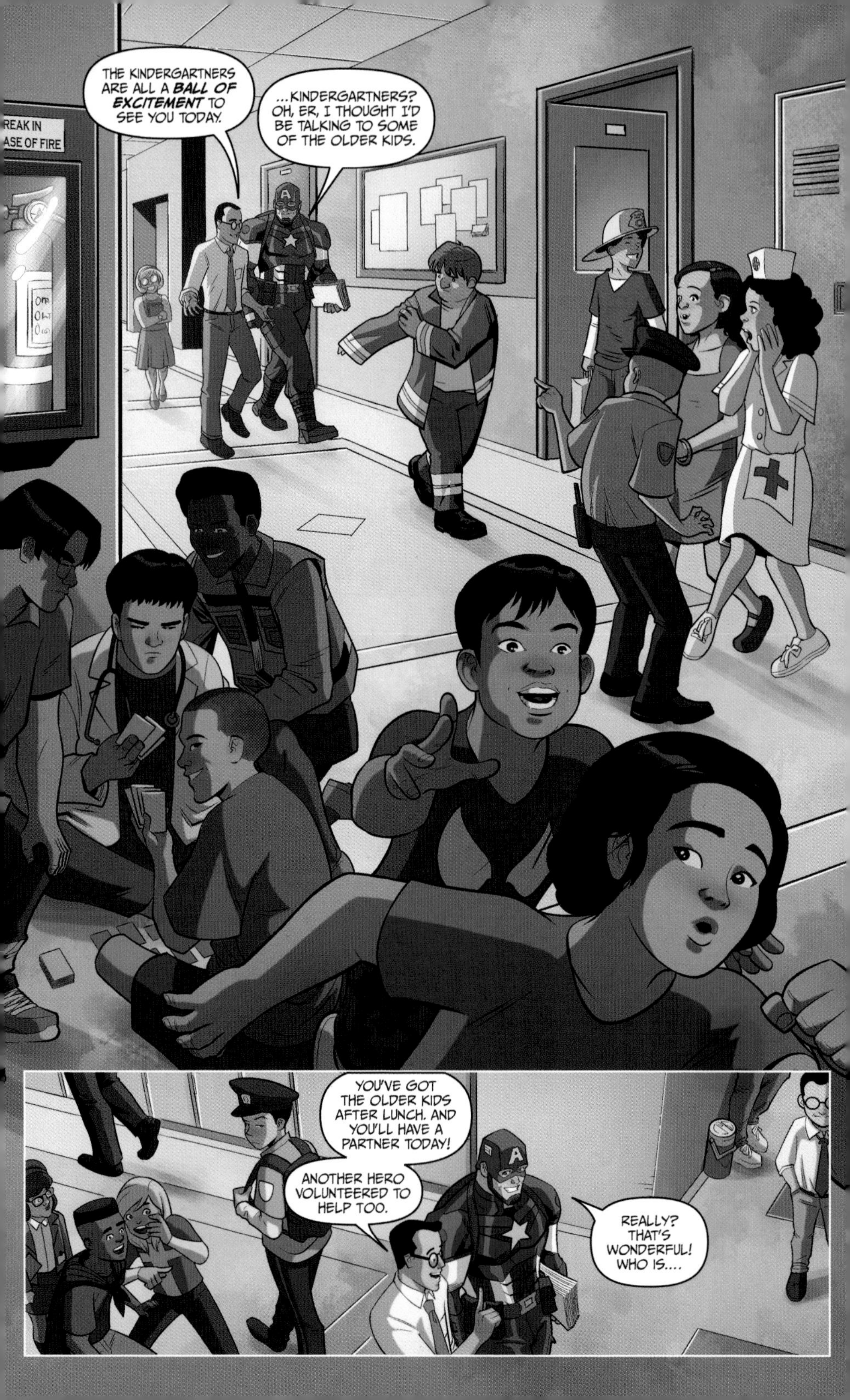
REAK IN
ASE OF FIRE
THE KINDERGARTNERS ARE ALL A **BALL OF EXCITEMENT** TO SEE YOU TODAY.
...KINDERGARTNERS? OH, ER, I THOUGHT I'D BE TALKING TO SOME OF THE OLDER KIDS.
YOU'VE GOT THE OLDER KIDS AFTER LUNCH. AND YOU'LL HAVE A PARTNER TODAY!
ANOTHER HERO VOLUNTEERED TO HELP TOO.
REALLY? THAT'S WONDERFUL! WHO IS....

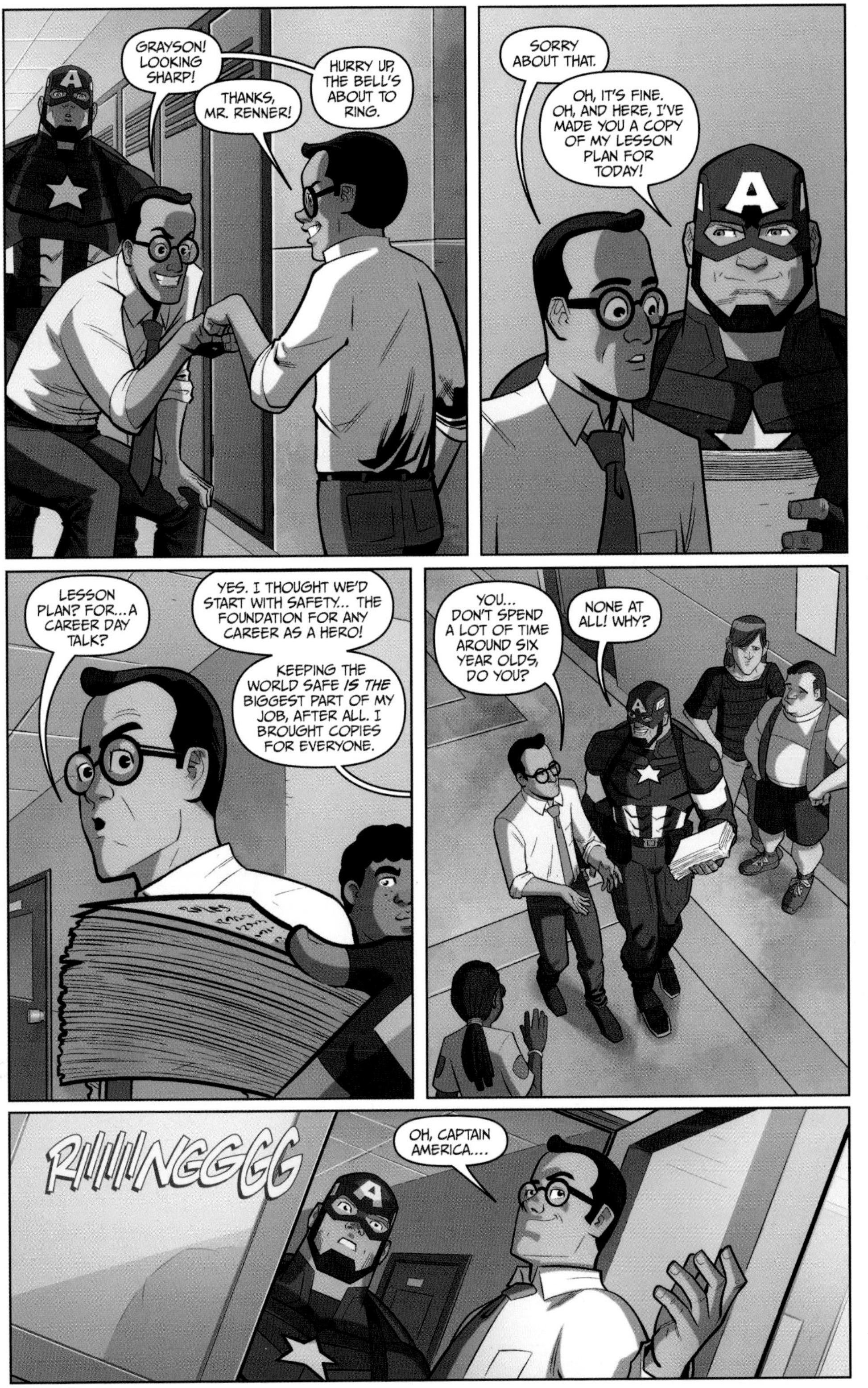
GRAYSON! LOOKING SHARP!
HURRY UP, THE BELL'S ABOUT TO RING.
THANKS, MR. RENNER!
SORRY ABOUT THAT.
OH, IT'S FINE. OH, AND HERE, I'VE MADE YOU A COPY OF MY LESSON PLAN FOR TODAY!
LESSON PLAN? FOR...A CAREER DAY TALK?
YES. I THOUGHT WE'D START WITH SAFETY... THE FOUNDATION FOR ANY CAREER AS A HERO!
KEEPING THE WORLD SAFE IS THE BIGGEST PART OF MY JOB, AFTER ALL. I BROUGHT COPIES FOR EVERYONE.
YOU... DON'T SPEND A LOT OF TIME AROUND SIX YEAR OLDS, DO YOU?
NONE AT ALL! WHY?
RIIIINGGGG
OH, CAPTAIN AMERICA....

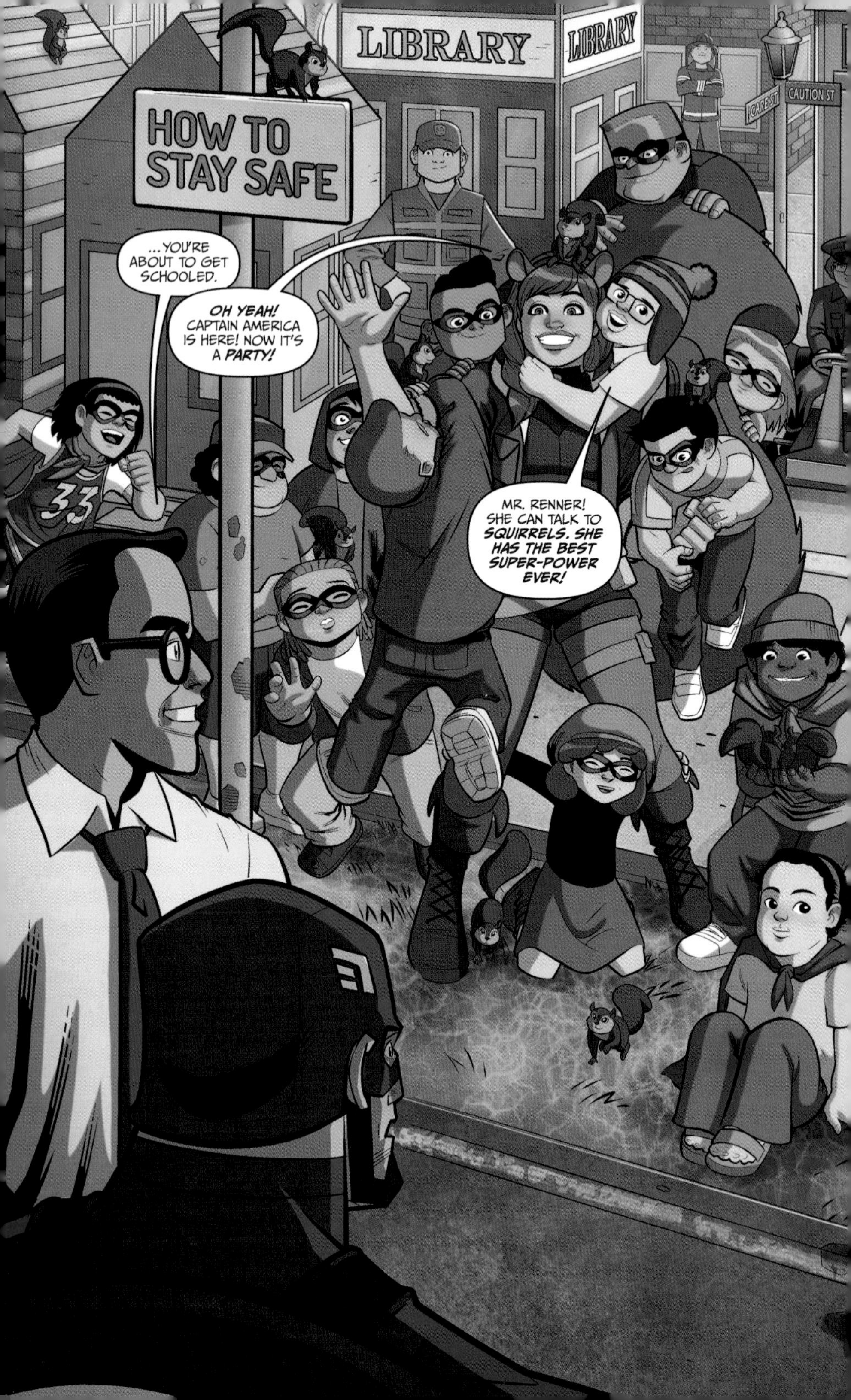
HOW TO STAY SAFE
LIBRARY
LIBRARY
CARE ST
CAUTION ST
...YOU'RE ABOUT TO GET SCHOOLED.
OH YEAH! CAPTAIN AMERICA IS HERE! NOW IT'S A PARTY!
MR. RENNER! SHE CAN TALK TO SQUIRRELS. SHE HAS THE BEST SUPER-POWER EVER!

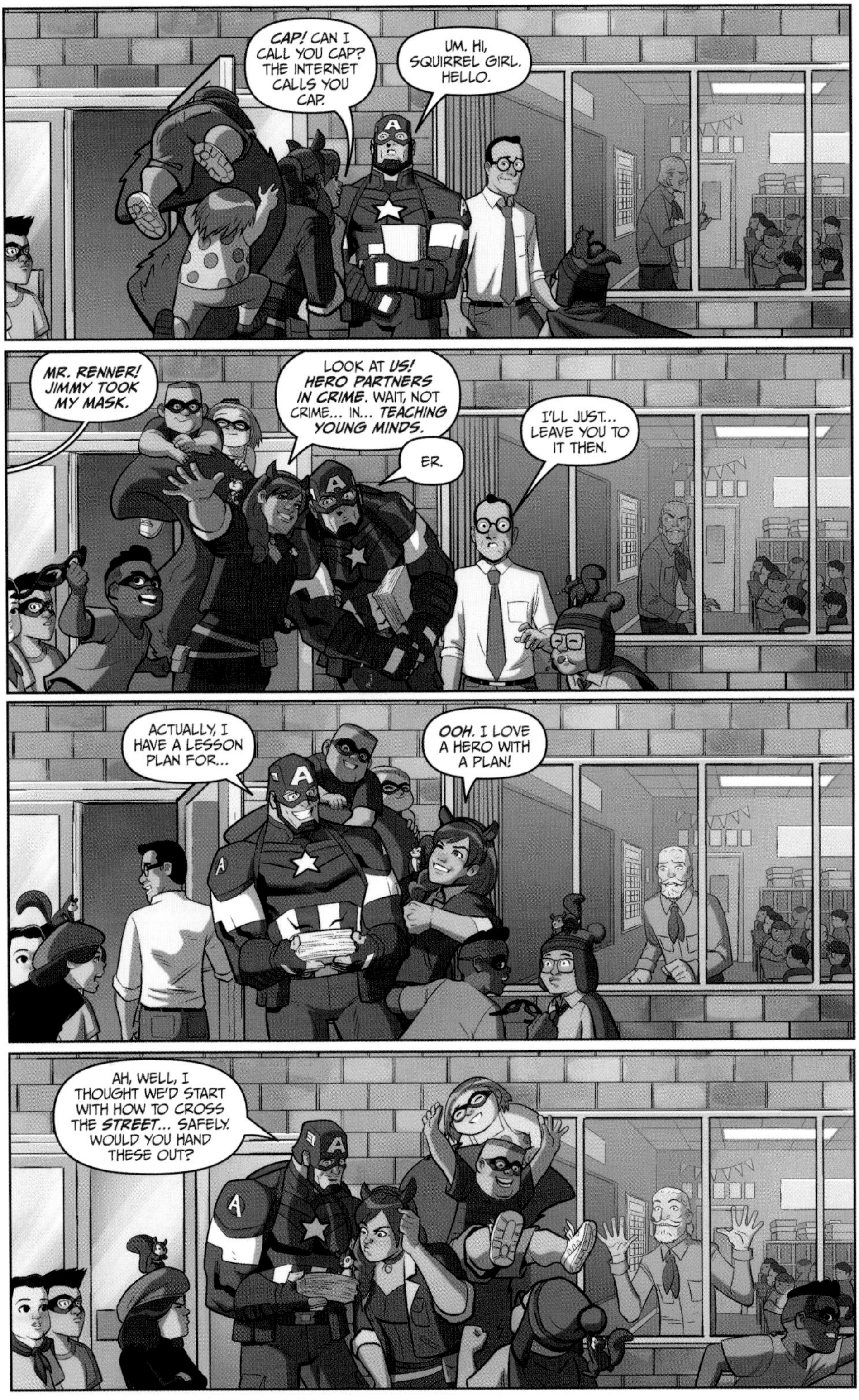
CAP! CAN I CALL YOU CAP? THE INTERNET CALLS YOU CAP.
UM. HI, SQUIRREL GIRL. HELLO.
MR. RENNER! JIMMY TOOK MY MASK.
LOOK AT US! HERO PARTNERS IN CRIME. WAIT, NOT CRIME... IN... TEACHING YOUNG MINDS.
ER.
I'LL JUST... LEAVE YOU TO IT THEN.
ACTUALLY, I HAVE A LESSON PLAN FOR...
OOH. I LOVE A HERO WITH A PLAN!
AH, WELL, I THOUGHT WE'D START WITH HOW TO CROSS THE STREET... SAFELY. WOULD YOU HAND THESE OUT?

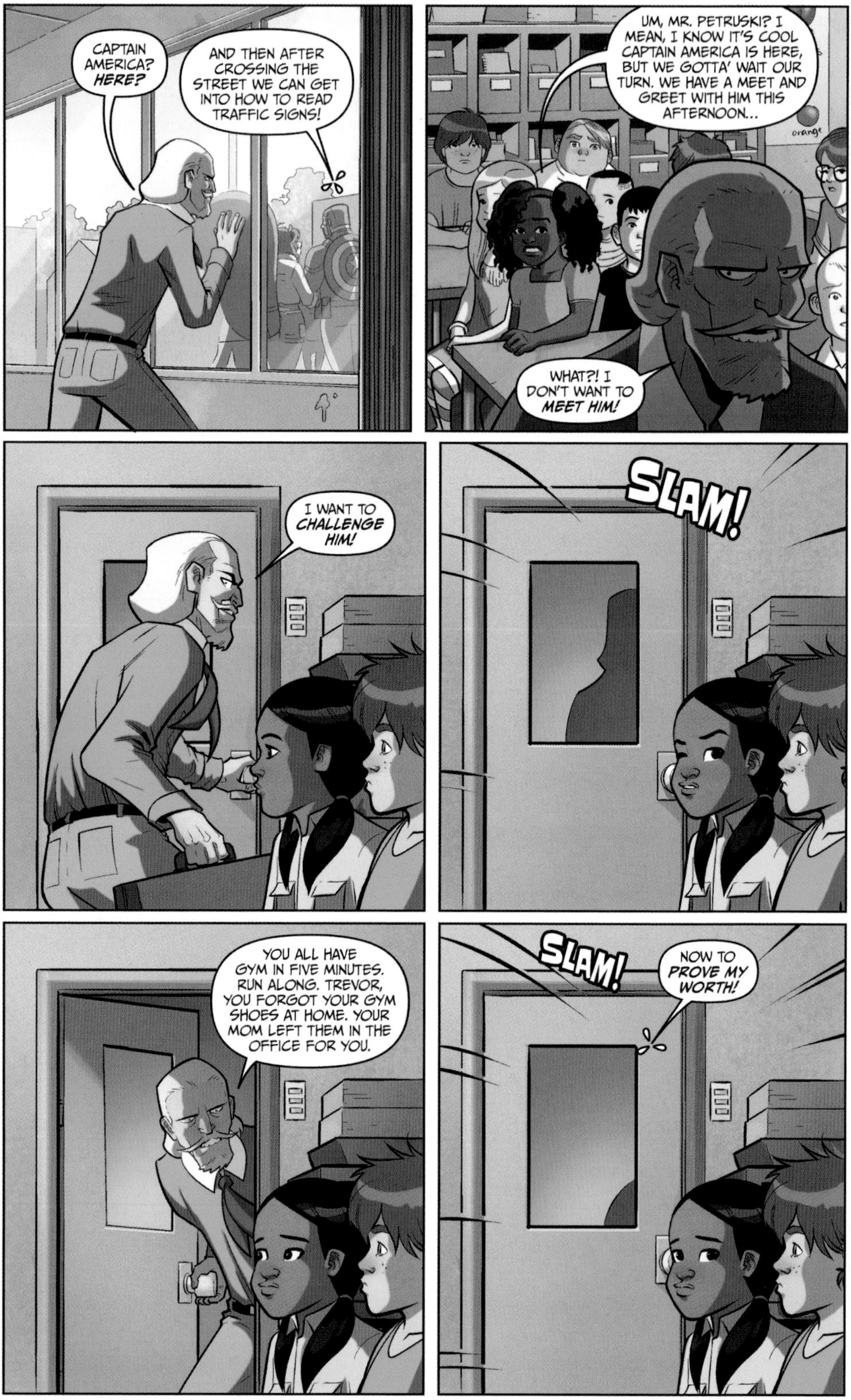
CAPTAIN AMERICA? HERE?
AND THEN AFTER CROSSING THE STREET WE CAN GET INTO HOW TO READ TRAFFIC SIGNS!
UM, MR. PETRUSKI? I MEAN, I KNOW IT'S COOL CAPTAIN AMERICA IS HERE, BUT WE GOTTA' WAIT OUR TURN. WE HAVE A MEET AND GREET WITH HIM THIS AFTERNOON...
orange
WHAT?! I DON'T WANT TO MEET HIM!
I WANT TO CHALLENGE HIM!
SLAM!
YOU ALL HAVE GYM IN FIVE MINUTES. RUN ALONG. TREVOR, YOU FORGOT YOUR GYM SHOES AT HOME. YOUR MOM LEFT THEM IN THE OFFICE FOR YOU.
SLAM!
NOW TO PROVE MY WORTH!

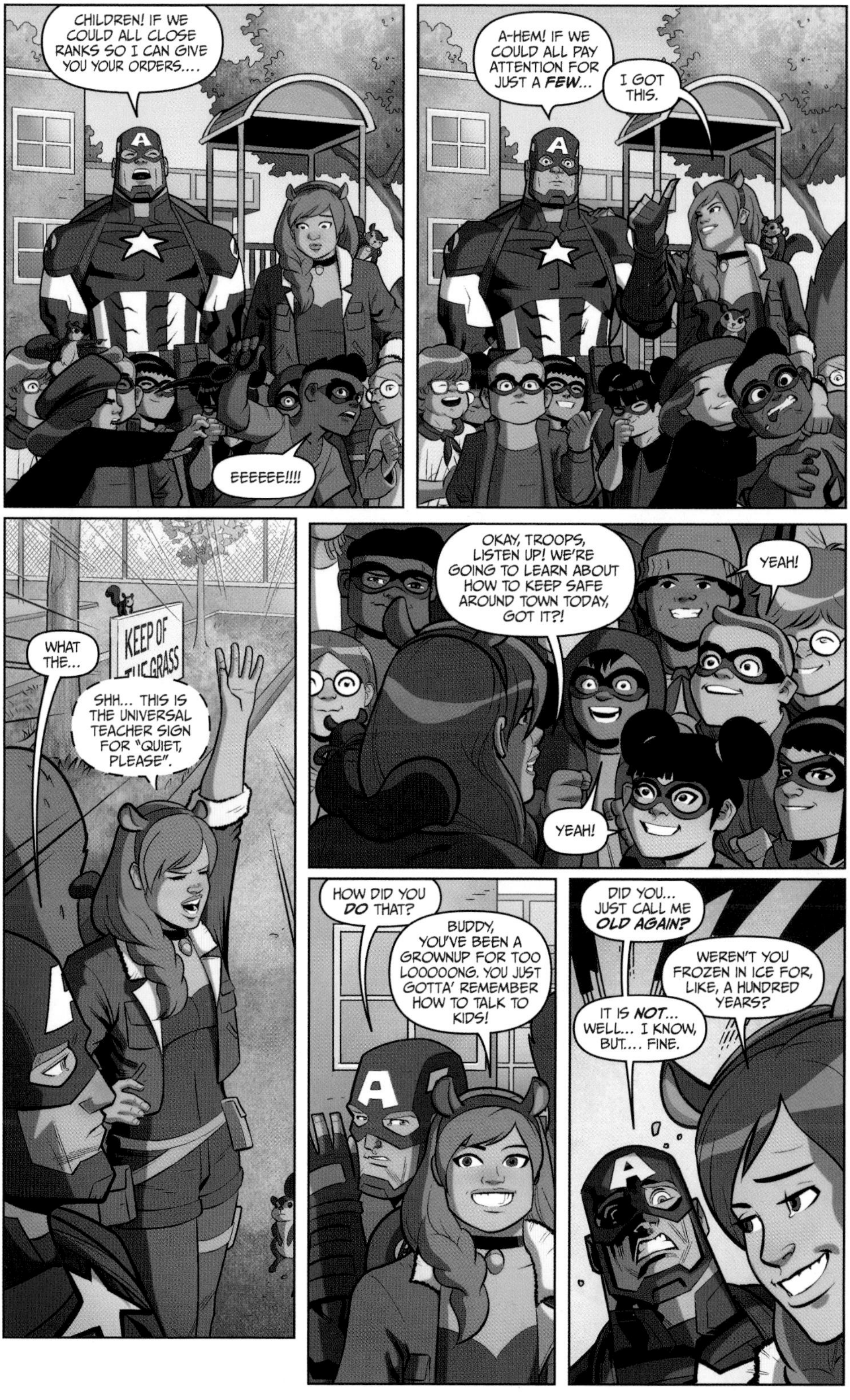
CHILDREN! IF WE COULD ALL CLOSE RANKS SO I CAN GIVE YOU YOUR ORDERS....
EEEEEE!!!!
A-HEM! IF WE COULD ALL PAY ATTENTION FOR JUST A *FEW*...
I GOT THIS.
KEEP OF
WHAT THE...
SHH... THIS IS THE UNIVERSAL TEACHER SIGN FOR "QUIET, PLEASE".
OKAY, TROOPS, LISTEN UP! WE'RE GOING TO LEARN ABOUT HOW TO KEEP SAFE AROUND TOWN TODAY, GOT IT?!
YEAH!
YEAH!
HOW DID YOU *DO* THAT?
BUDDY, YOU'VE BEEN A GROWNUP FOR TOO LOOOOONG. YOU JUST GOTTA' REMEMBER HOW TO TALK TO KIDS!
DID YOU... JUST CALL ME *OLD AGAIN?*
WEREN'T YOU FROZEN IN ICE FOR, LIKE, A HUNDRED YEARS?
IT IS *NOT*... WELL... I KNOW, BUT.... FINE.

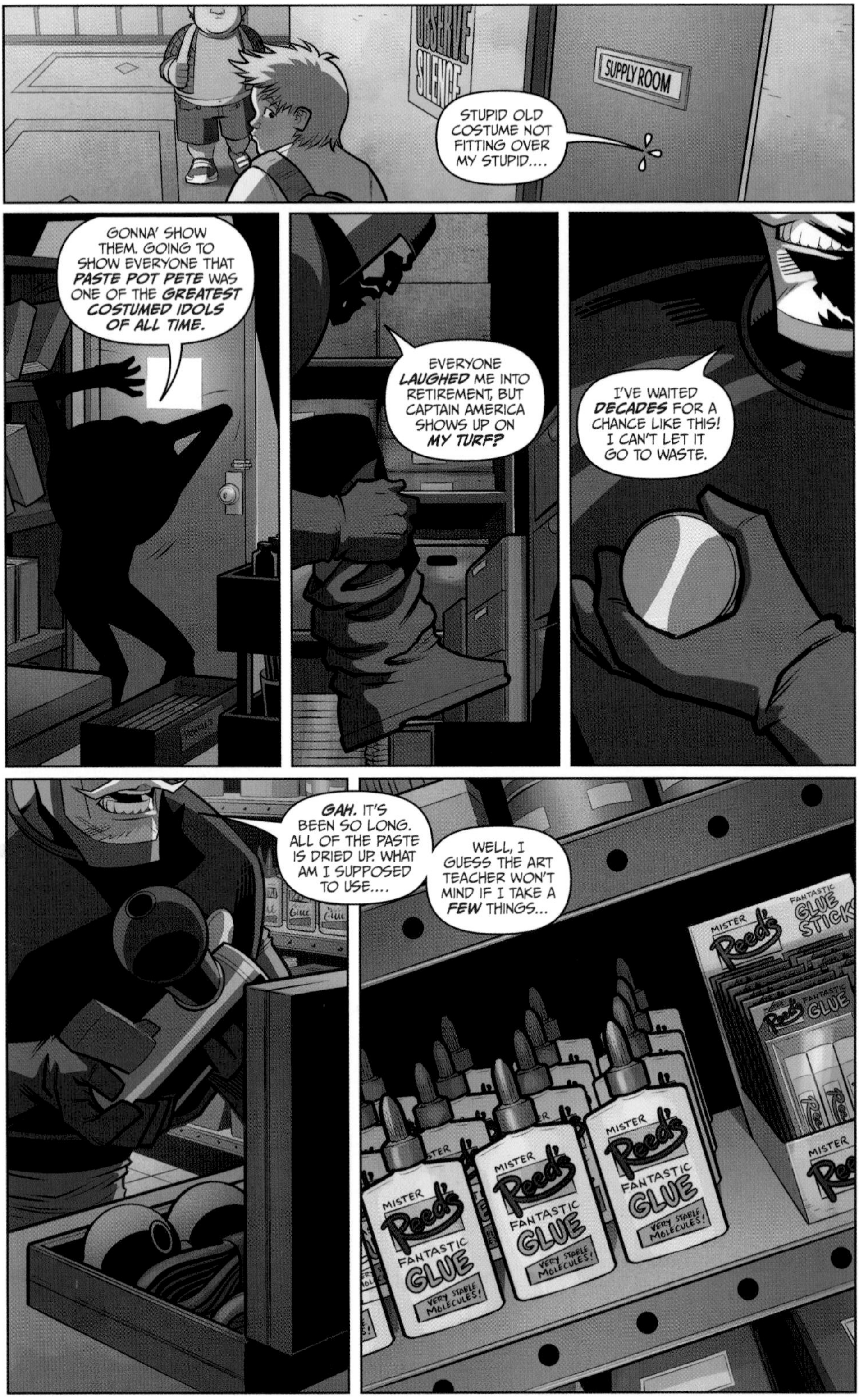
OBSERVE SILENCE
SUPPLY ROOM
STUPID OLD COSTUME NOT FITTING OVER MY STUPID....
GONNA' SHOW THEM. GOING TO SHOW EVERYONE THAT PASTE POT PETE WAS ONE OF THE GREATEST COSTUMED IDOLS OF ALL TIME.
PENCILS
EVERYONE LAUGHED ME INTO RETIREMENT, BUT CAPTAIN AMERICA SHOWS UP ON MY TURF?
I'VE WAITED DECADES FOR A CHANCE LIKE THIS! I CAN'T LET IT GO TO WASTE.
GAH. IT'S BEEN SO LONG. ALL OF THE PASTE IS DRIED UP. WHAT AM I SUPPOSED TO USE....
WELL, I GUESS THE ART TEACHER WON'T MIND IF I TAKE A FEW THINGS...
MISTER Reed's FANTASTIC GLUE STICKS
MISTER Reed's FANTASTIC GLUE
VERY STABLE MOLECULES!

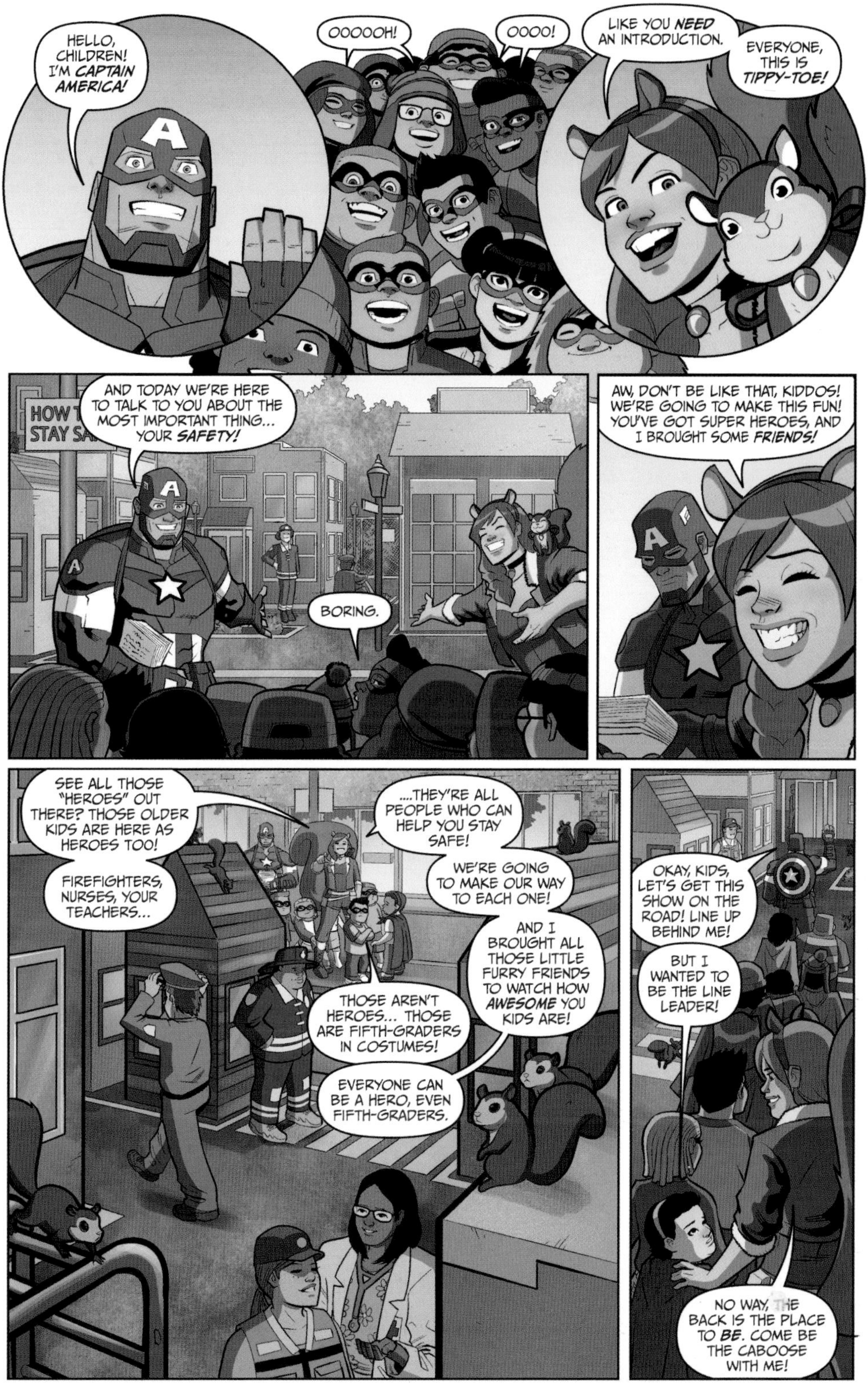
HELLO, CHILDREN! I'M CAPTAIN AMERICA!
OOOOOH!
OOOO!
LIKE YOU NEED AN INTRODUCTION.
EVERYONE, THIS IS TIPPY-TOE!
HOW T
STAY SA
AND TODAY WE'RE HERE TO TALK TO YOU ABOUT THE MOST IMPORTANT THING... YOUR SAFETY!
BORING.
AW, DON'T BE LIKE THAT, KIDDOS! WE'RE GOING TO MAKE THIS FUN! YOU'VE GOT SUPER HEROES, AND I BROUGHT SOME FRIENDS!
SEE ALL THOSE "HEROES" OUT THERE? THOSE OLDER KIDS ARE HERE AS HEROES TOO!
FIREFIGHTERS, NURSES, YOUR TEACHERS...
....THEY'RE ALL PEOPLE WHO CAN HELP YOU STAY SAFE!
WE'RE GOING TO MAKE OUR WAY TO EACH ONE!
AND I BROUGHT ALL THOSE LITTLE FURRY FRIENDS TO WATCH HOW AWESOME YOU KIDS ARE!
THOSE AREN'T HEROES... THOSE ARE FIFTH-GRADERS IN COSTUMES!
EVERYONE CAN BE A HERO, EVEN FIFTH-GRADERS.
OKAY, KIDS, LET'S GET THIS SHOW ON THE ROAD! LINE UP BEHIND ME!
BUT I WANTED TO BE THE LINE LEADER!
NO WAY, THE BACK IS THE PLACE TO BE. COME BE THE CABOOSE WITH ME!

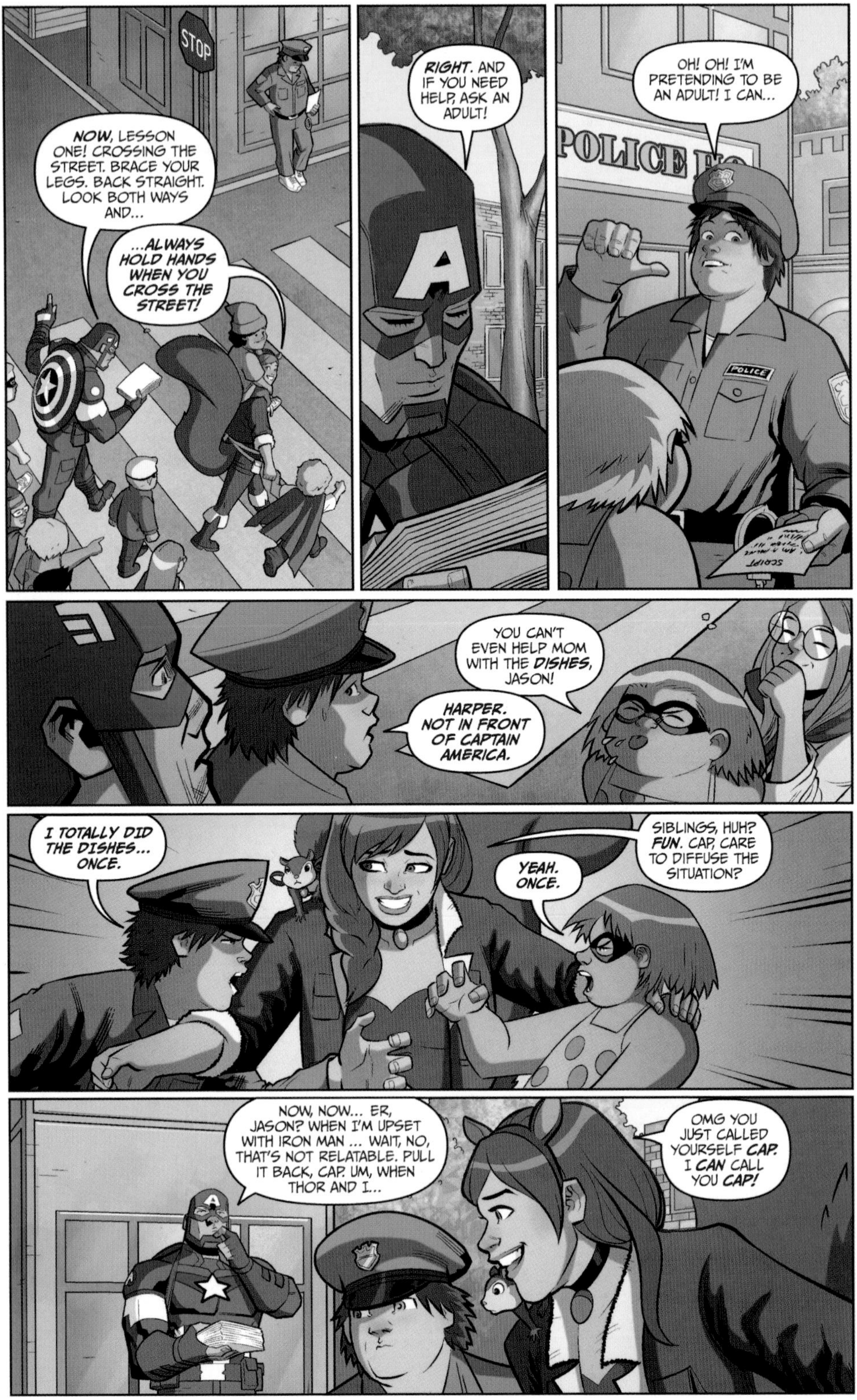

STOP
NOW, LESSON ONE! CROSSING THE STREET. BRACE YOUR LEGS. BACK STRAIGHT. LOOK BOTH WAYS AND...
...ALWAYS HOLD HANDS WHEN YOU CROSS THE STREET!
RIGHT. AND IF YOU NEED HELP, ASK AN ADULT!
OH! OH! I'M PRETENDING TO BE AN ADULT! I CAN...
POLICE
POLICE
SCRIPT
YOU CAN'T EVEN HELP MOM WITH THE DISHES, JASON!
HARPER. NOT IN FRONT OF CAPTAIN AMERICA.
I TOTALLY DID THE DISHES... ONCE.
YEAH. ONCE.
SIBLINGS, HUH? FUN. CAP, CARE TO DIFFUSE THE SITUATION?
NOW, NOW... ER, JASON? WHEN I'M UPSET WITH IRON MAN ... WAIT, NO, THAT'S NOT RELATABLE. PULL IT BACK, CAP. UM, WHEN THOR AND I...
OMG YOU JUST CALLED YOURSELF CAP. I CAN CALL YOU CAP!

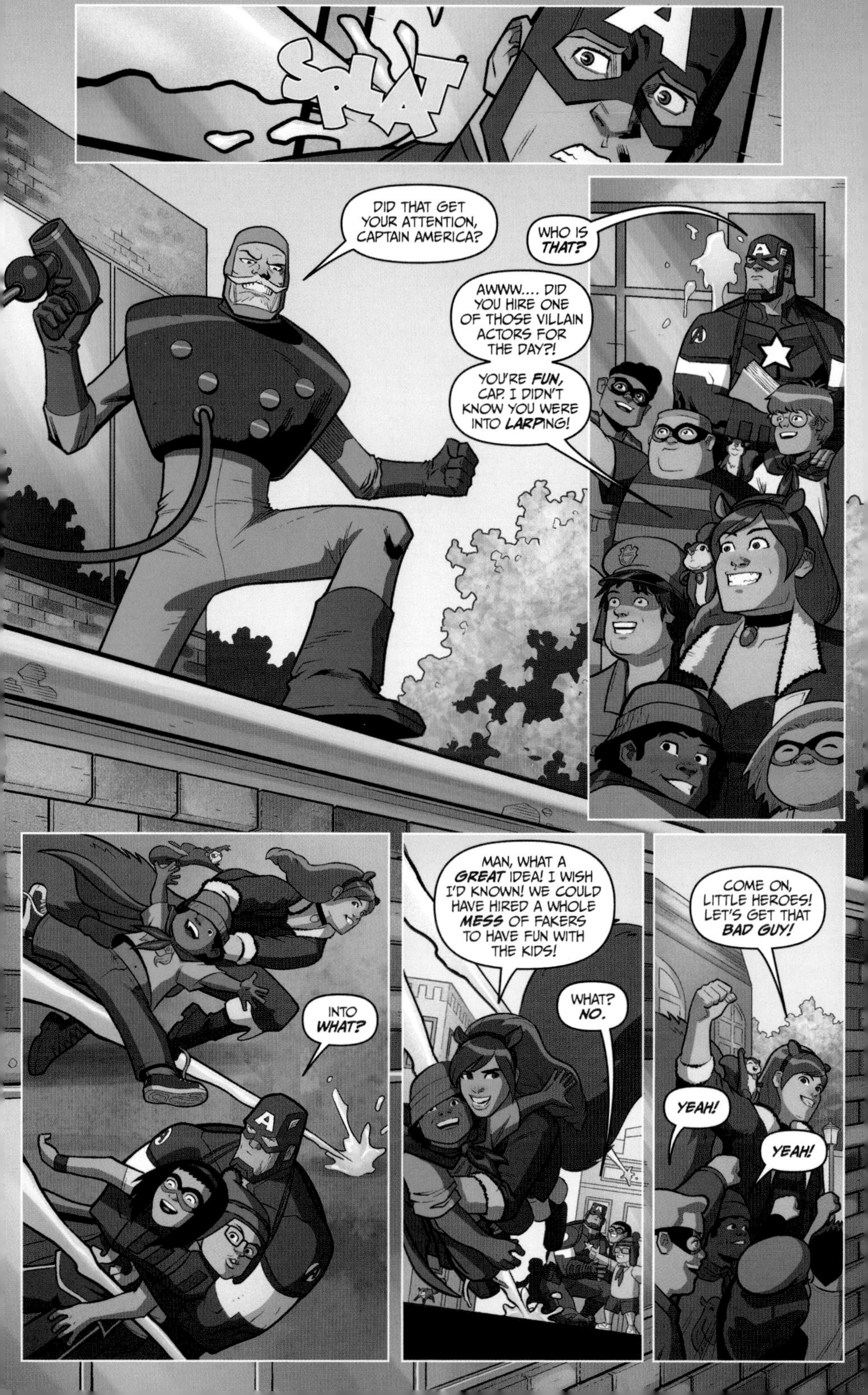
SPLAT
DID THAT GET YOUR ATTENTION, CAPTAIN AMERICA?
WHO IS THAT?
AWWW.... DID YOU HIRE ONE OF THOSE VILLAIN ACTORS FOR THE DAY?!
YOU'RE FUN, CAP. I DIDN'T KNOW YOU WERE INTO LARPING!
INTO WHAT?
MAN, WHAT A GREAT IDEA! I WISH I'D KNOWN! WE COULD HAVE HIRED A WHOLE MESS OF FAKERS TO HAVE FUN WITH THE KIDS!
WHAT? NO.
COME ON, LITTLE HEROES! LET'S GET THAT BAD GUY!
YEAH!
YEAH!

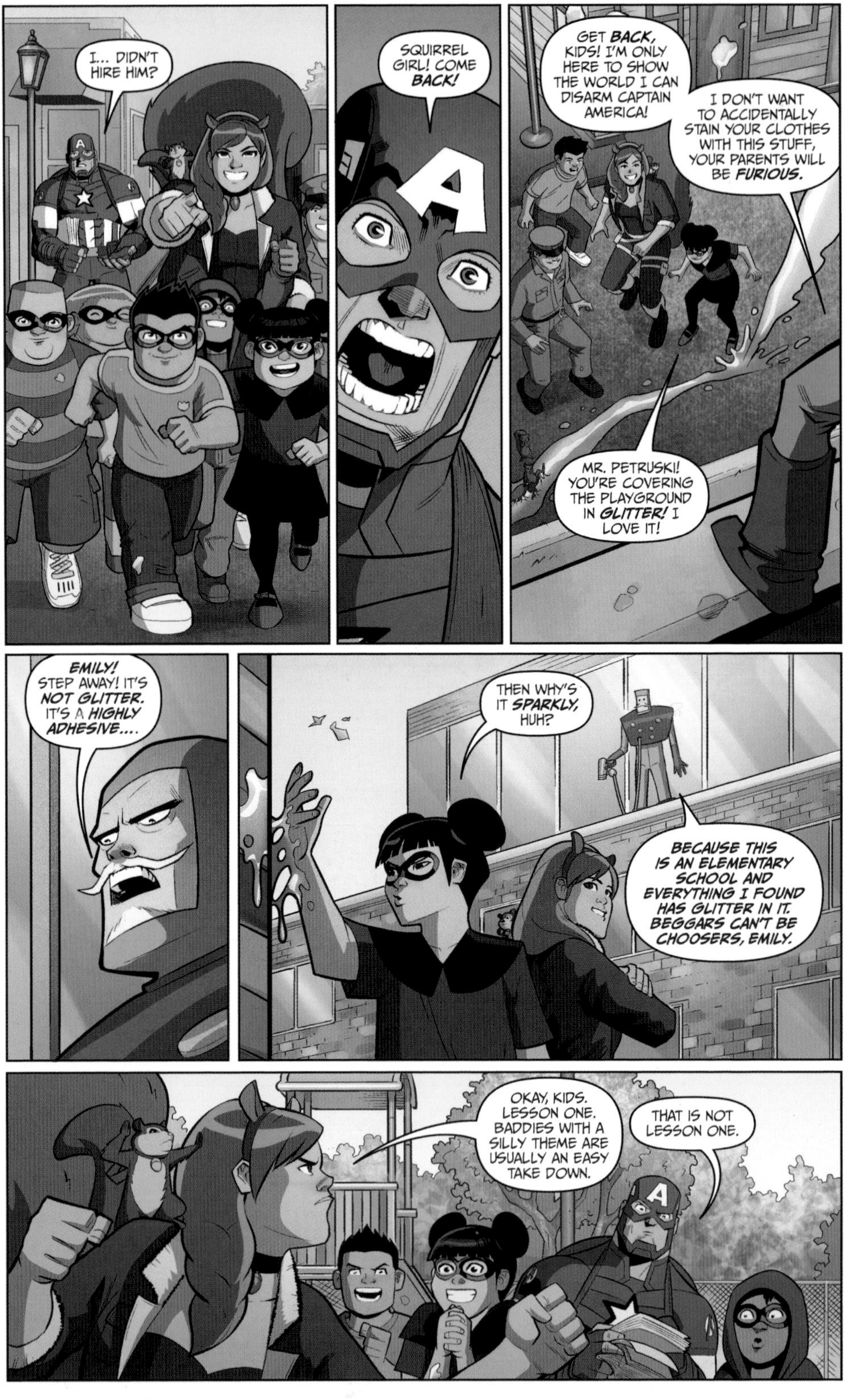
I... DIDN'T HIRE HIM?
SQUIRREL GIRL! COME BACK!
GET BACK, KIDS! I'M ONLY HERE TO SHOW THE WORLD I CAN DISARM CAPTAIN AMERICA!
I DON'T WANT TO ACCIDENTALLY STAIN YOUR CLOTHES WITH THIS STUFF, YOUR PARENTS WILL BE FURIOUS.
MR. PETRUSKI! YOU'RE COVERING THE PLAYGROUND IN GLITTER! I LOVE IT!
EMILY! STEP AWAY! IT'S NOT GLITTER. IT'S A HIGHLY ADHESIVE....
THEN WHY'S IT SPARKLY, HUH?
BECAUSE THIS IS AN ELEMENTARY SCHOOL AND EVERYTHING I FOUND HAS GLITTER IN IT. BEGGARS CAN'T BE CHOOSERS, EMILY.
OKAY, KIDS. LESSON ONE. BADDIES WITH A SILLY THEME ARE USUALLY AN EASY TAKE DOWN.
THAT IS NOT LESSON ONE.

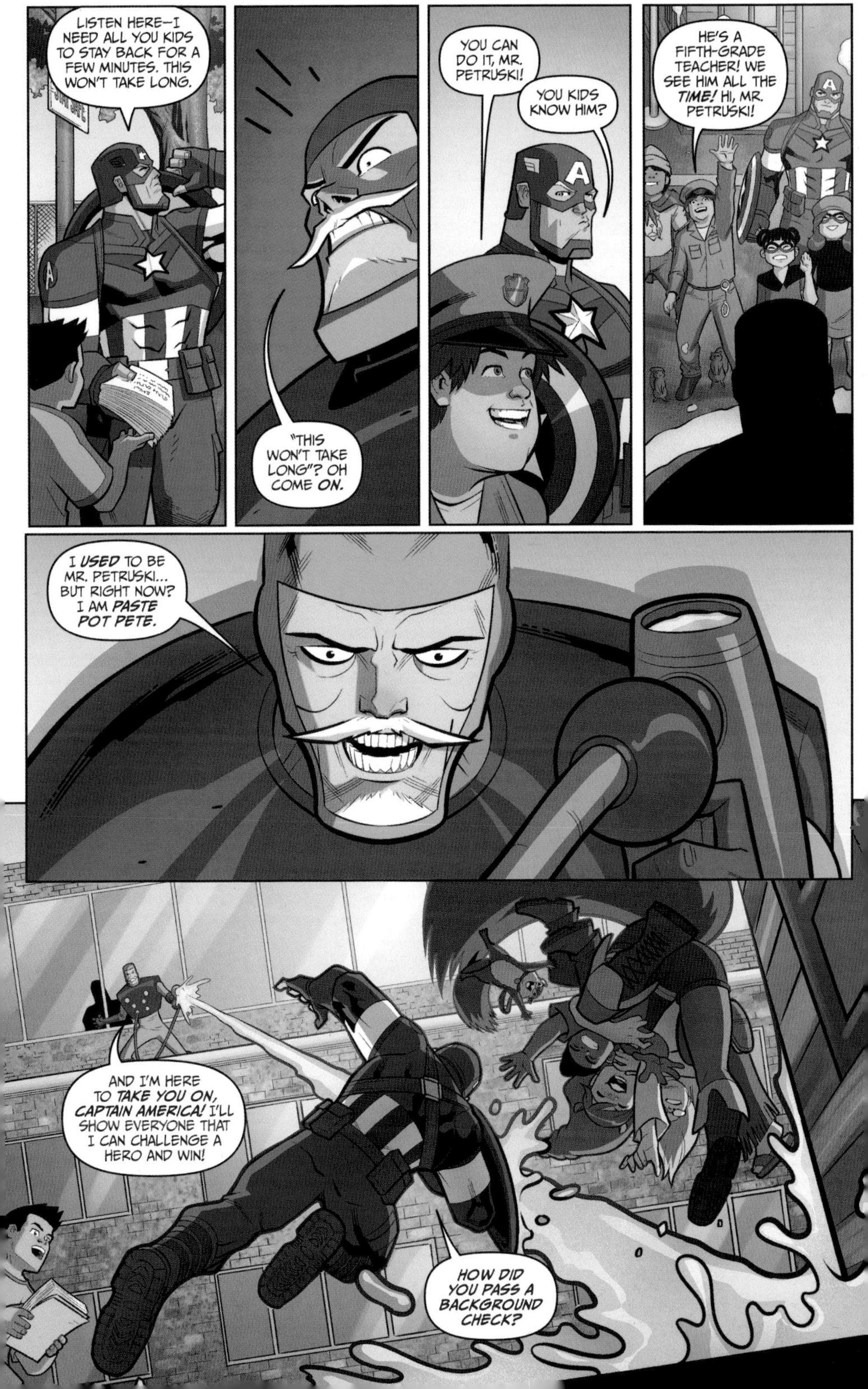
LISTEN HERE—I NEED ALL YOU KIDS TO STAY BACK FOR A FEW MINUTES. THIS WON'T TAKE LONG.
"THIS WON'T TAKE LONG"? OH COME ON.
YOU CAN DO IT, MR. PETRUSKI!
YOU KIDS KNOW HIM?
HE'S A FIFTH-GRADE TEACHER! WE SEE HIM ALL THE TIME! HI, MR. PETRUSKI!
I USED TO BE MR. PETRUSKI... BUT RIGHT NOW? I AM PASTE POT PETE.
AND I'M HERE TO TAKE YOU ON, CAPTAIN AMERICA! I'LL SHOW EVERYONE THAT I CAN CHALLENGE A HERO AND WIN!
HOW DID YOU PASS A BACKGROUND CHECK?

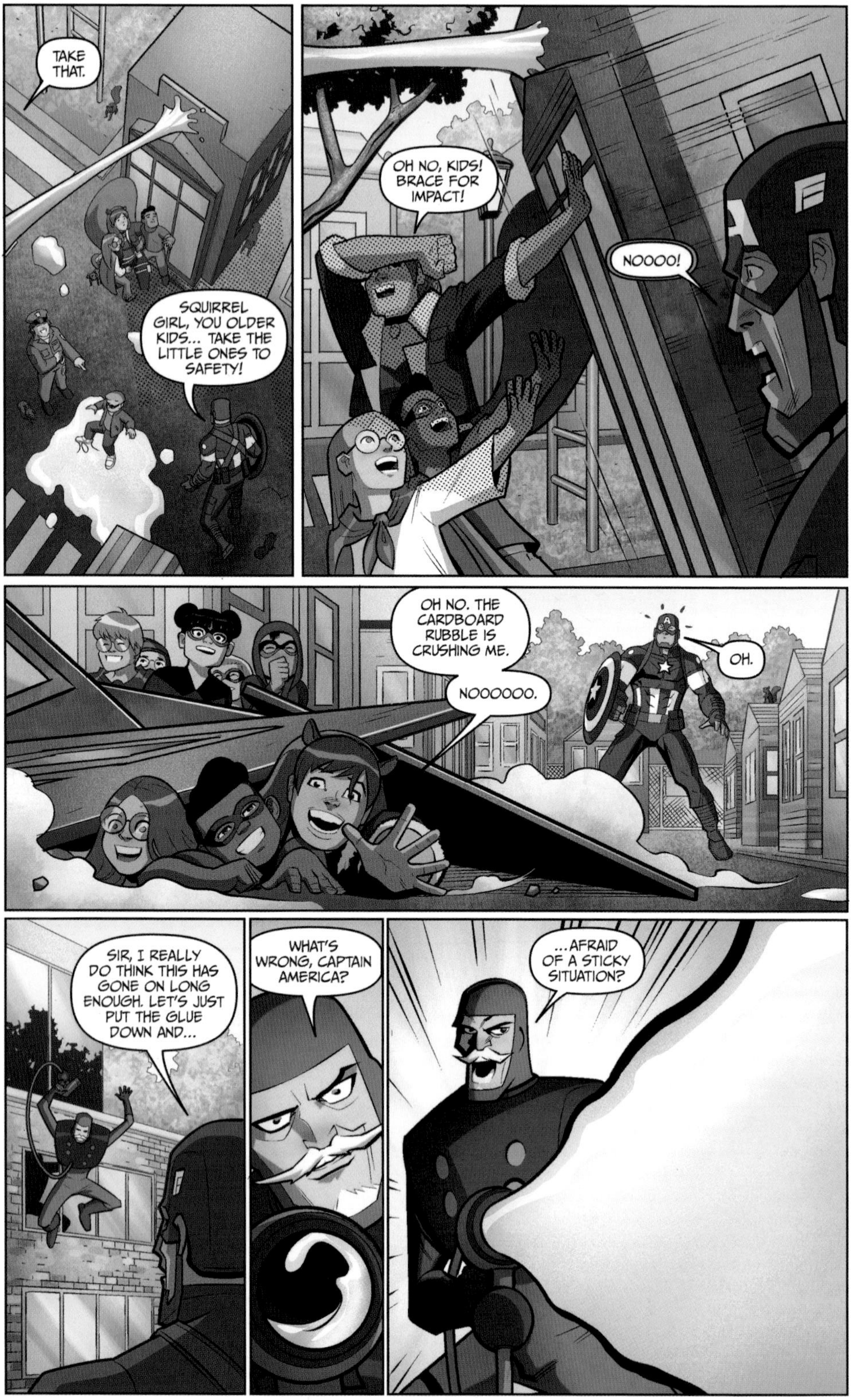
TAKE THAT.
SQUIRREL GIRL, YOU OLDER KIDS... TAKE THE LITTLE ONES TO SAFETY!
OH NO, KIDS! BRACE FOR IMPACT!
NOOOO!
OH NO. THE CARDBOARD RUBBLE IS CRUSHING ME.
NOOOOOO.
OH.
SIR, I REALLY DO THINK THIS HAS GONE ON LONG ENOUGH. LET'S JUST PUT THE GLUE DOWN AND...
WHAT'S WRONG, CAPTAIN AMERICA?
...AFRAID OF A STICKY SITUATION?

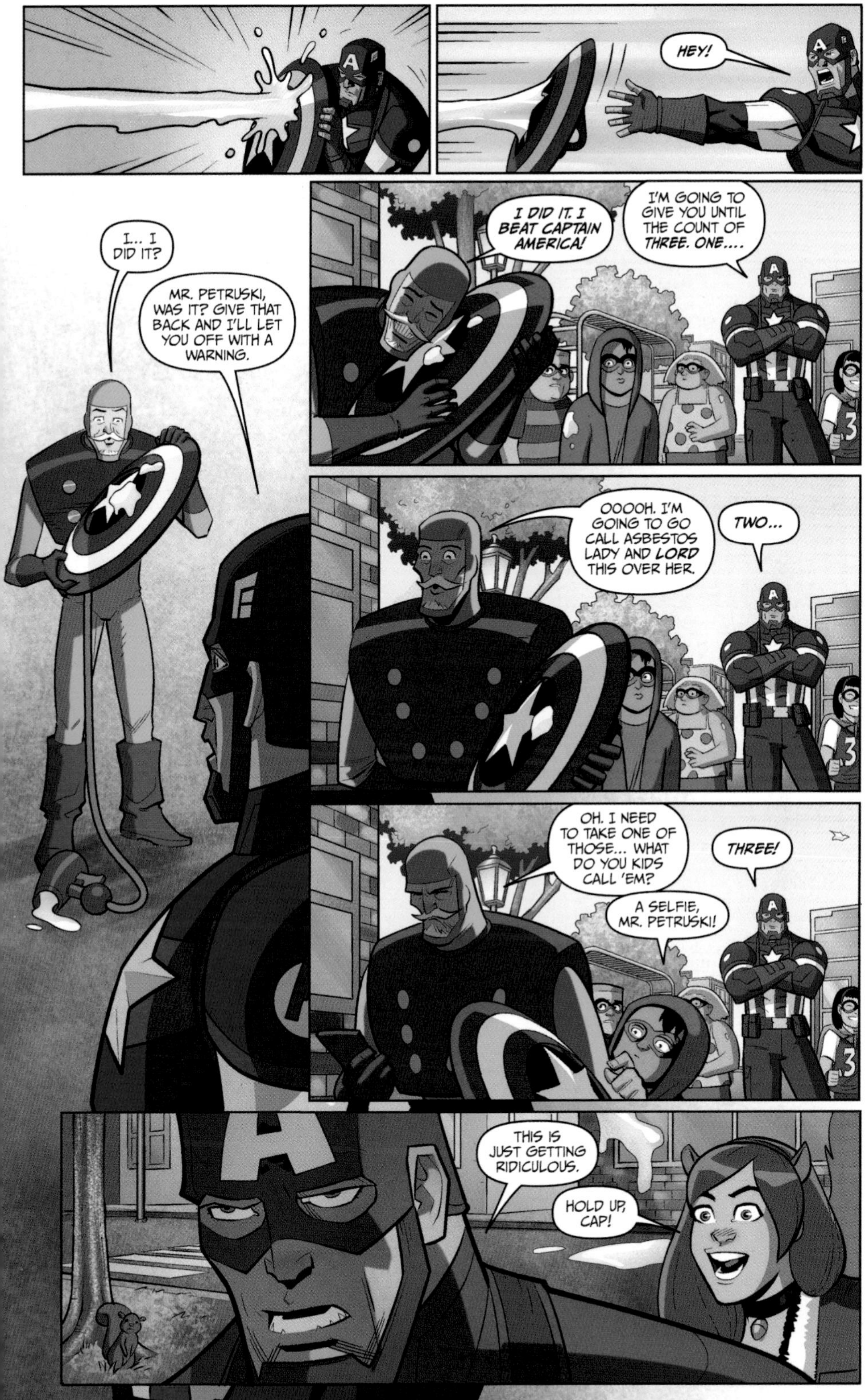
HEY!
I... I DID IT?
MR. PETRUSKI, WAS IT? GIVE THAT BACK AND I'LL LET YOU OFF WITH A WARNING.
I DID IT. I BEAT CAPTAIN AMERICA!
I'M GOING TO GIVE YOU UNTIL THE COUNT OF THREE. ONE....
OOOOH. I'M GOING TO GO CALL ASBESTOS LADY AND LORD THIS OVER HER.
TWO...
OH. I NEED TO TAKE ONE OF THOSE... WHAT DO YOU KIDS CALL 'EM?
A SELFIE, MR. PETRUSKI!
THREE!
THIS IS JUST GETTING RIDICULOUS.
HOLD UP, CAP!

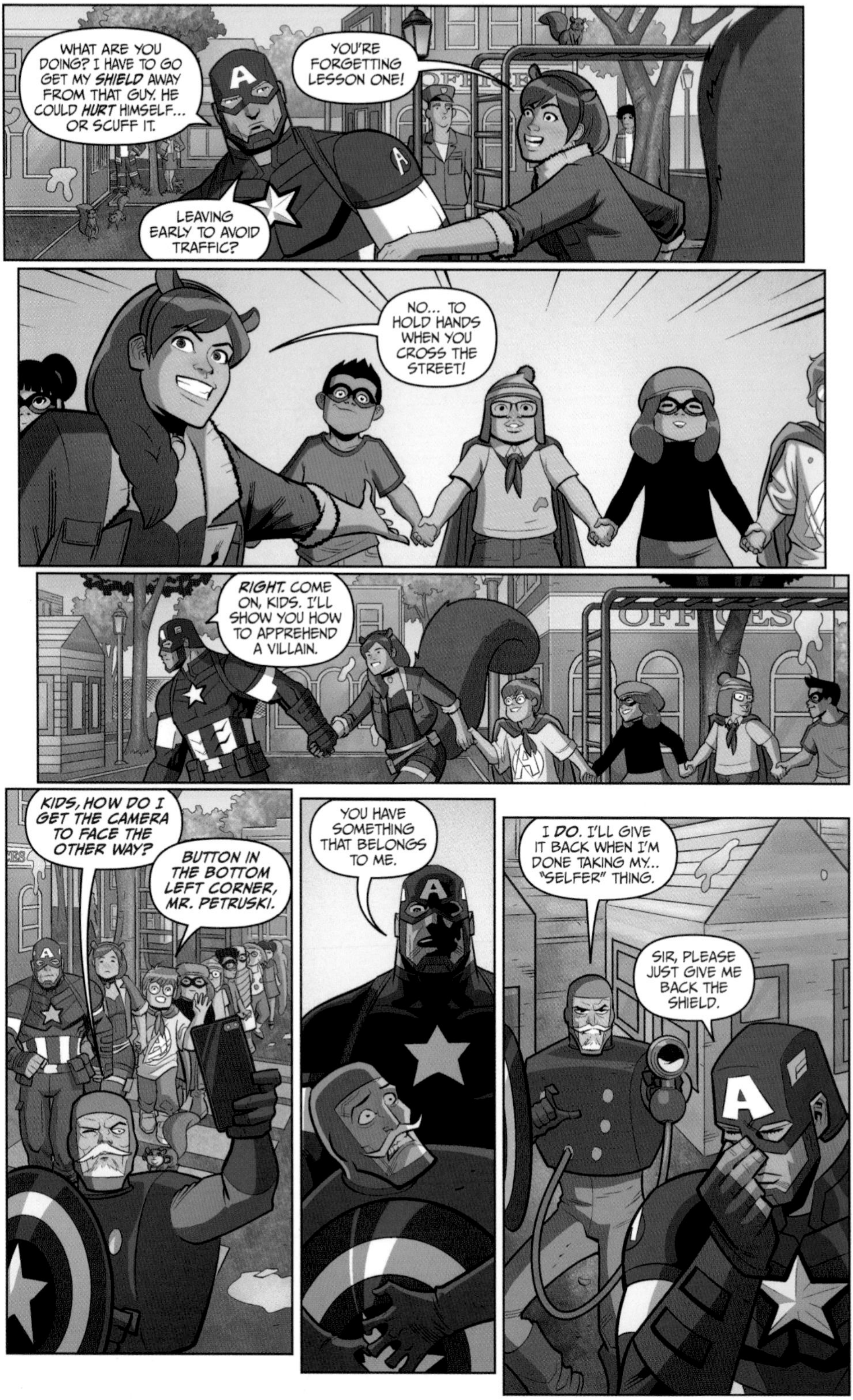
WHAT ARE YOU DOING? I HAVE TO GO GET MY SHIELD AWAY FROM THAT GUY. HE COULD HURT HIMSELF... OR SCUFF IT.
YOU'RE FORGETTING LESSON ONE!
LEAVING EARLY TO AVOID TRAFFIC?
NO... TO HOLD HANDS WHEN YOU CROSS THE STREET!
RIGHT. COME ON, KIDS. I'LL SHOW YOU HOW TO APPREHEND A VILLAIN.
OFFICES
KIDS, HOW DO I GET THE CAMERA TO FACE THE OTHER WAY?
BUTTON IN THE BOTTOM LEFT CORNER, MR. PETRUSKI.
YOU HAVE SOMETHING THAT BELONGS TO ME.
I DO. I'LL GIVE IT BACK WHEN I'M DONE TAKING MY... "SELFER" THING.
SIR, PLEASE JUST GIVE ME BACK THE SHIELD.

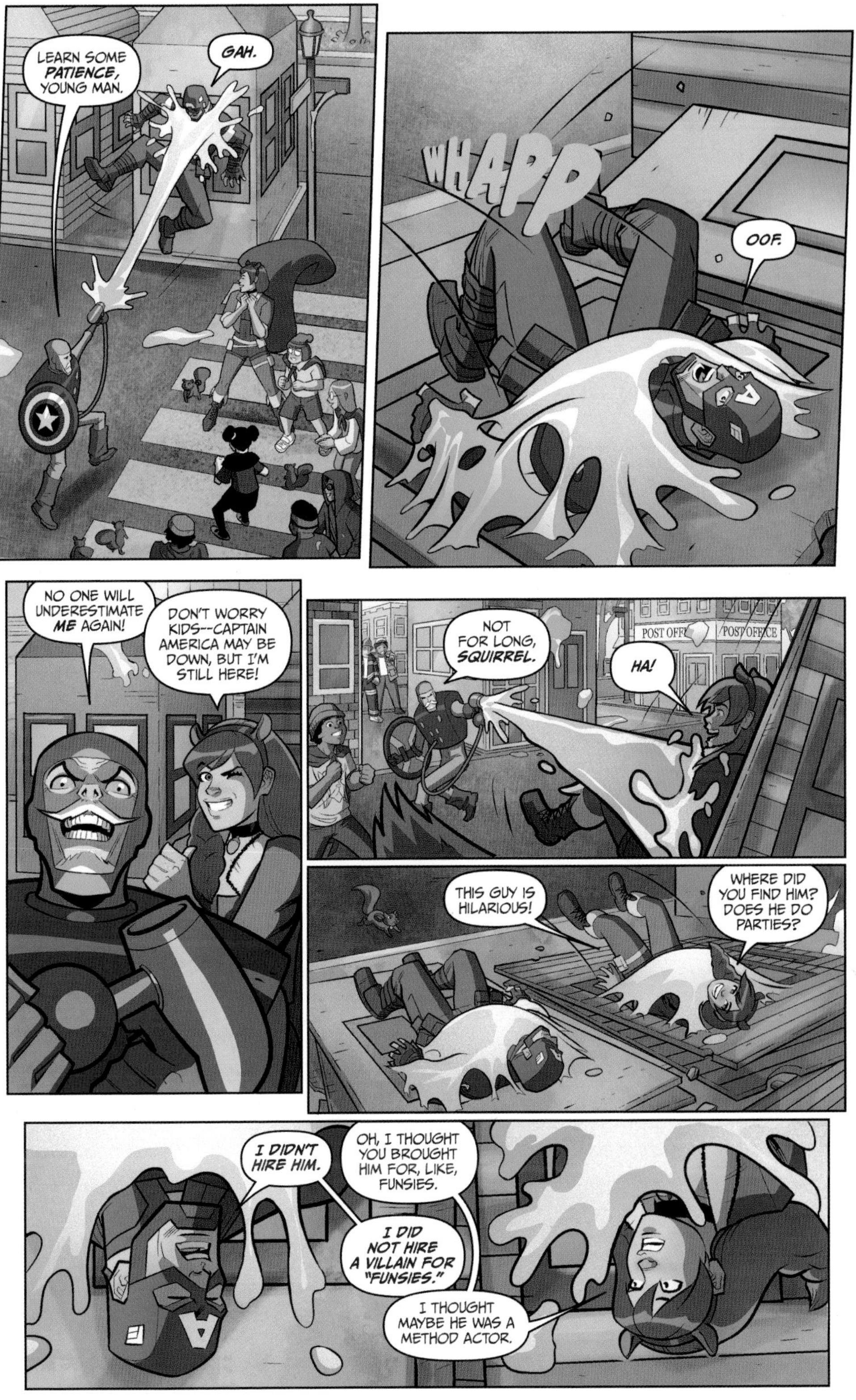
LEARN SOME PATIENCE, YOUNG MAN.
GAH.
WHAPP
OOF.
NO ONE WILL UNDERESTIMATE ME AGAIN!
DON'T WORRY KIDS--CAPTAIN AMERICA MAY BE DOWN, BUT I'M STILL HERE!
NOT FOR LONG, SQUIRREL.
HA!
POST OFFICE
THIS GUY IS HILARIOUS!
WHERE DID YOU FIND HIM? DOES HE DO PARTIES?
I DIDN'T HIRE HIM.
OH, I THOUGHT YOU BROUGHT HIM FOR, LIKE, FUNSIES.
I DID NOT HIRE A VILLAIN FOR "FUNSIES."
I THOUGHT MAYBE HE WAS A METHOD ACTOR.

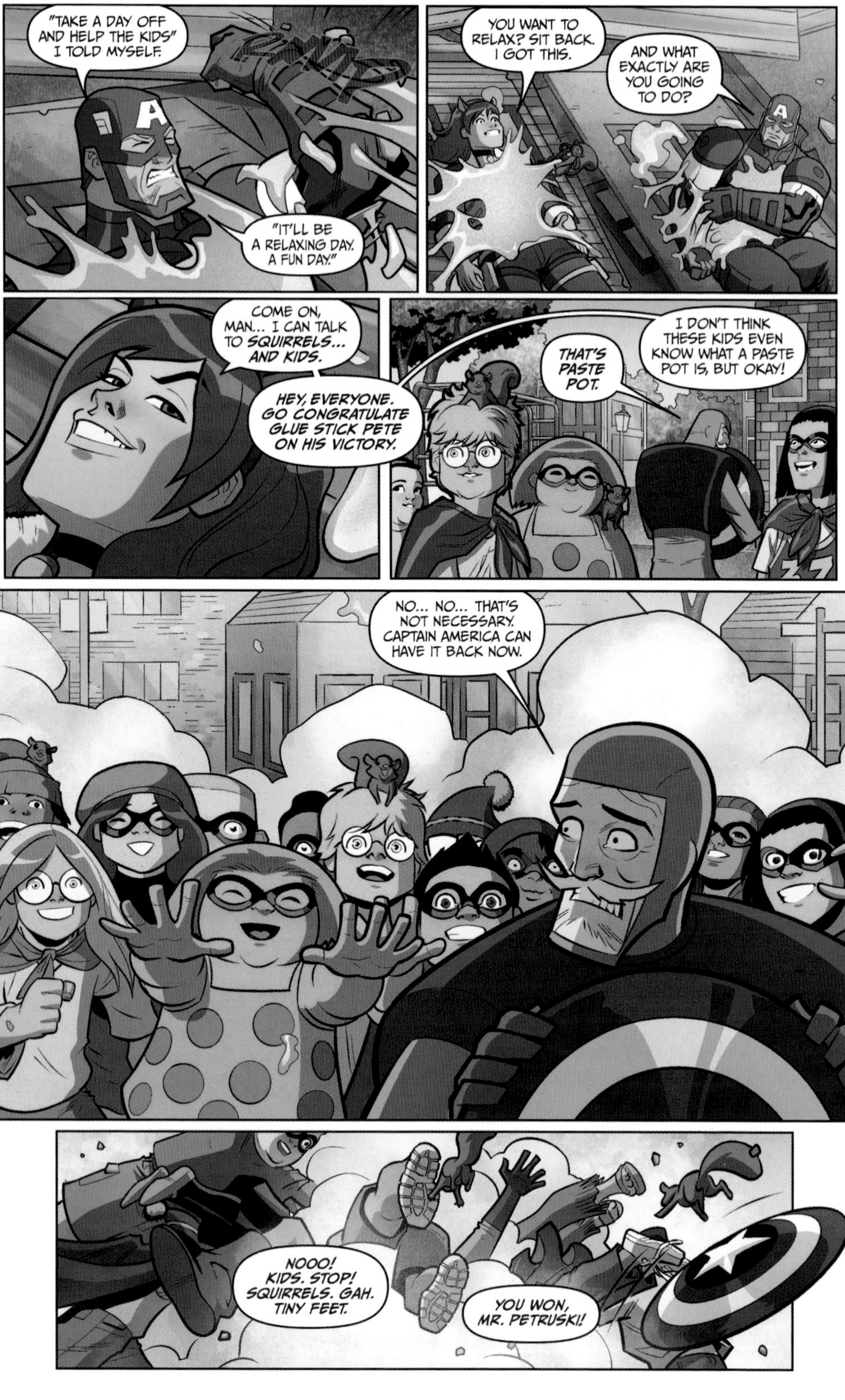
"TAKE A DAY OFF AND HELP THE KIDS" I TOLD MYSELF.
"IT'LL BE A RELAXING DAY. A FUN DAY."
YOU WANT TO RELAX? SIT BACK. I GOT THIS.
AND WHAT EXACTLY ARE YOU GOING TO DO?
COME ON, MAN... I CAN TALK TO SQUIRRELS... AND KIDS.
HEY, EVERYONE. GO CONGRATULATE GLUE STICK PETE ON HIS VICTORY.
THAT'S PASTE POT.
I DON'T THINK THESE KIDS EVEN KNOW WHAT A PASTE POT IS, BUT OKAY!
NO... NO... THAT'S NOT NECESSARY. CAPTAIN AMERICA CAN HAVE IT BACK NOW.
NOOO! KIDS. STOP! SQUIRRELS. GAH. TINY FEET.
YOU WON, MR. PETRUSKI!

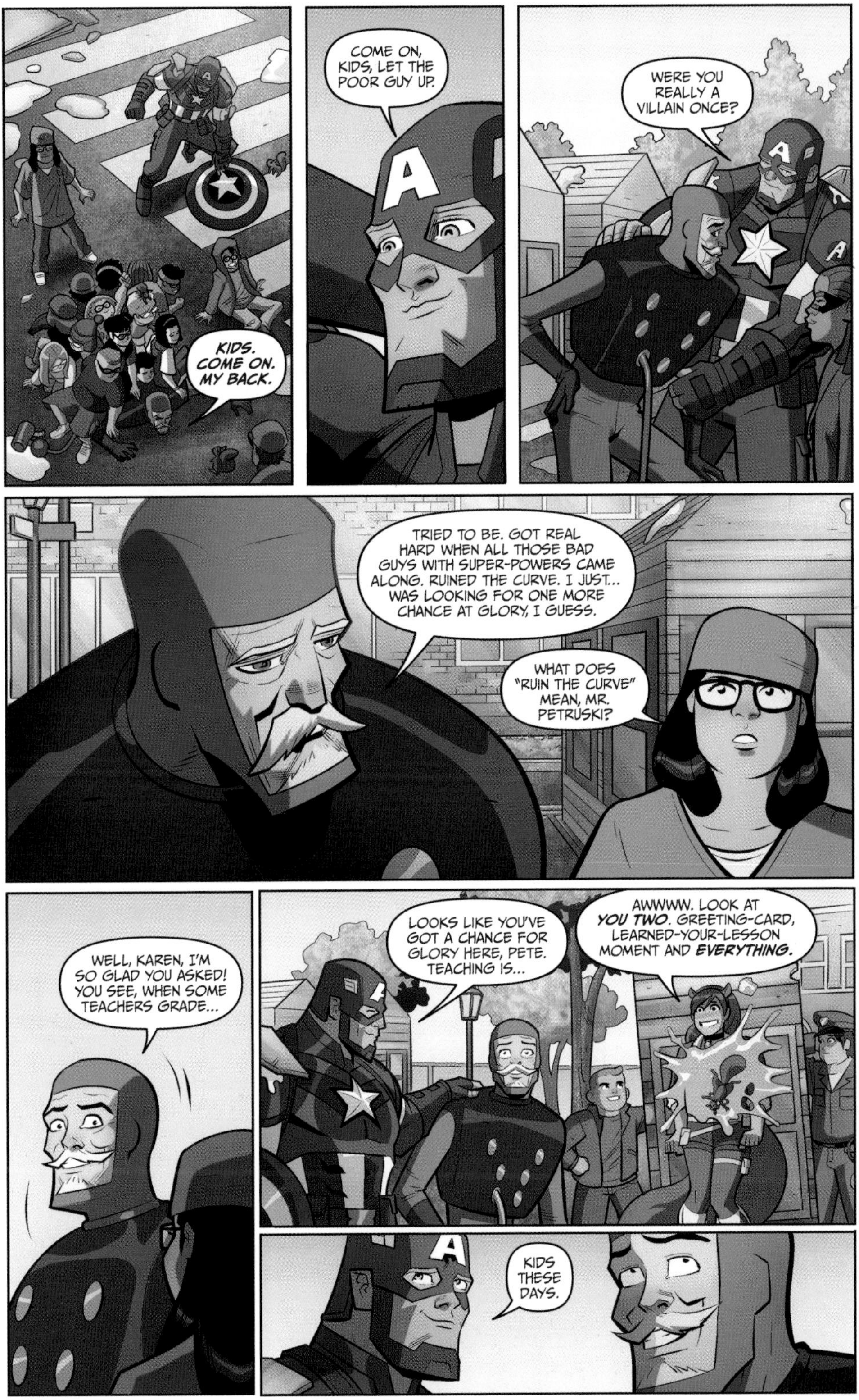
KIDS. COME ON. MY BACK.
COME ON, KIDS, LET THE POOR GUY UP.
WERE YOU REALLY A VILLAIN ONCE?
TRIED TO BE. GOT REAL HARD WHEN ALL THOSE BAD GUYS WITH SUPER-POWERS CAME ALONG. RUINED THE CURVE. I JUST... WAS LOOKING FOR ONE MORE CHANCE AT GLORY, I GUESS.
WHAT DOES "RUIN THE CURVE" MEAN, MR. PETRUSKI?
WELL, KAREN, I'M SO GLAD YOU ASKED! YOU SEE, WHEN SOME TEACHERS GRADE...
LOOKS LIKE YOU'VE GOT A CHANCE FOR GLORY HERE, PETE. TEACHING IS...
AWWWW. LOOK AT YOU TWO. GREETING-CARD, LEARNED-YOUR-LESSON MOMENT AND EVERYTHING.
KIDS THESE DAYS.

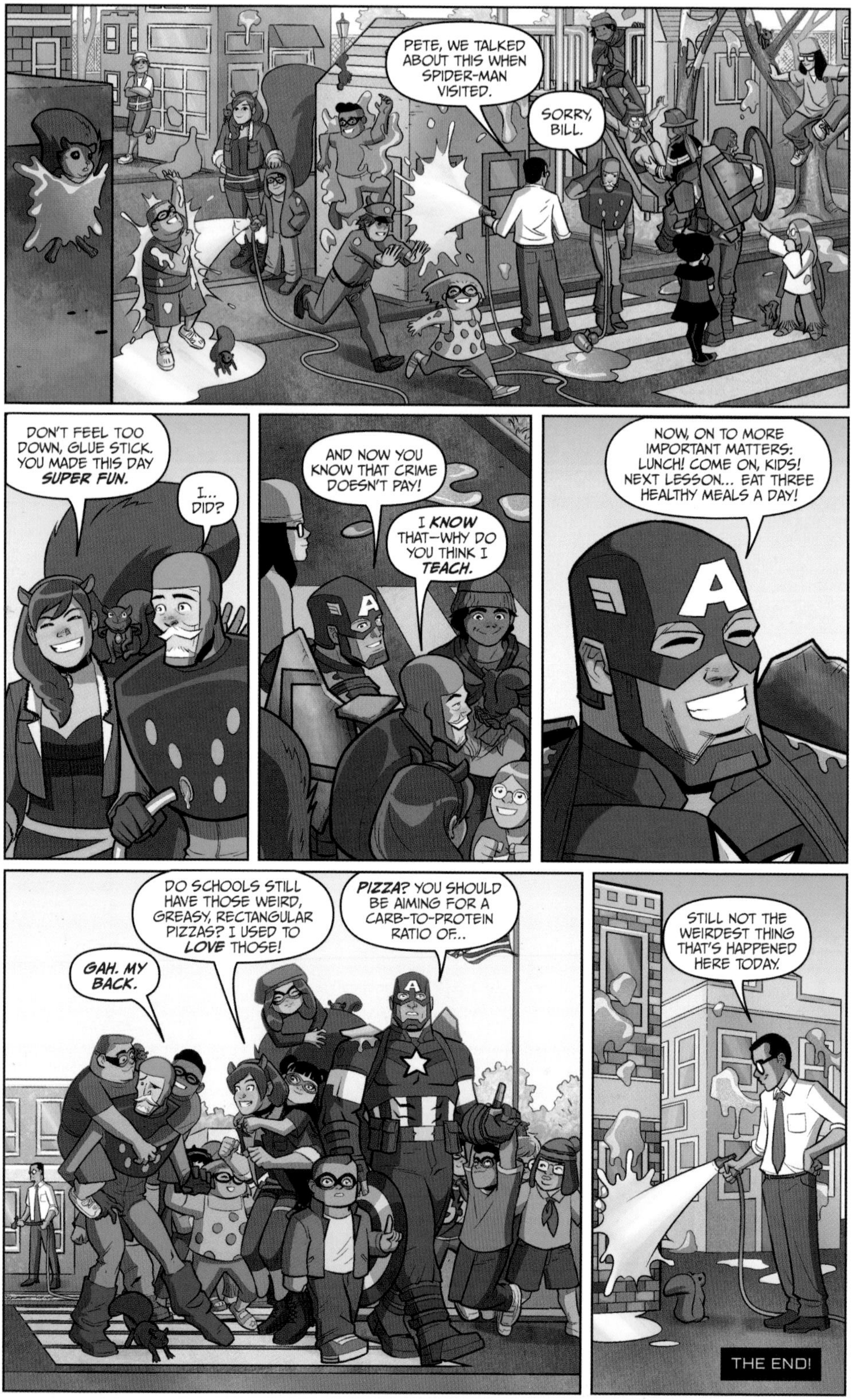
PETE, WE TALKED ABOUT THIS WHEN SPIDER-MAN VISITED.
SORRY, BILL.
DON'T FEEL TOO DOWN, GLUE STICK. YOU MADE THIS DAY SUPER FUN.
I... DID?
AND NOW YOU KNOW THAT CRIME DOESN'T PAY!
I KNOW THAT—WHY DO YOU THINK I TEACH.
NOW, ON TO MORE IMPORTANT MATTERS: LUNCH! COME ON, KIDS! NEXT LESSON... EAT THREE HEALTHY MEALS A DAY!
GAH. MY BACK.
DO SCHOOLS STILL HAVE THOSE WEIRD, GREASY, RECTANGULAR PIZZAS? I USED TO LOVE THOSE!
PIZZA? YOU SHOULD BE AIMING FOR A CARB-TO-PROTEIN RATIO OF...
STILL NOT THE WEIRDEST THING THAT'S HAPPENED HERE TODAY.
THE END!

ART BY: DENIS MEDRI

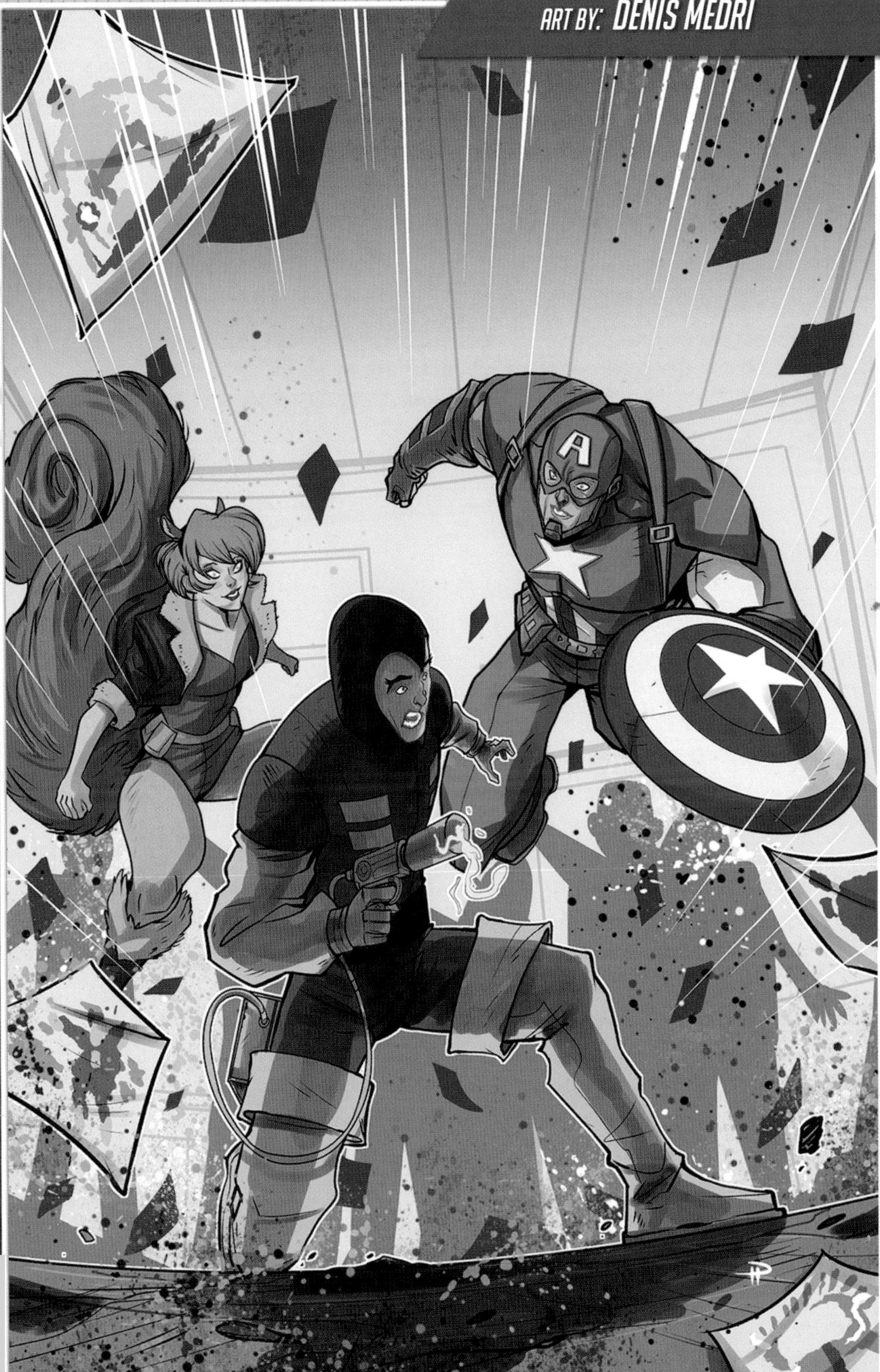

ART BY: BUTCH MAPA

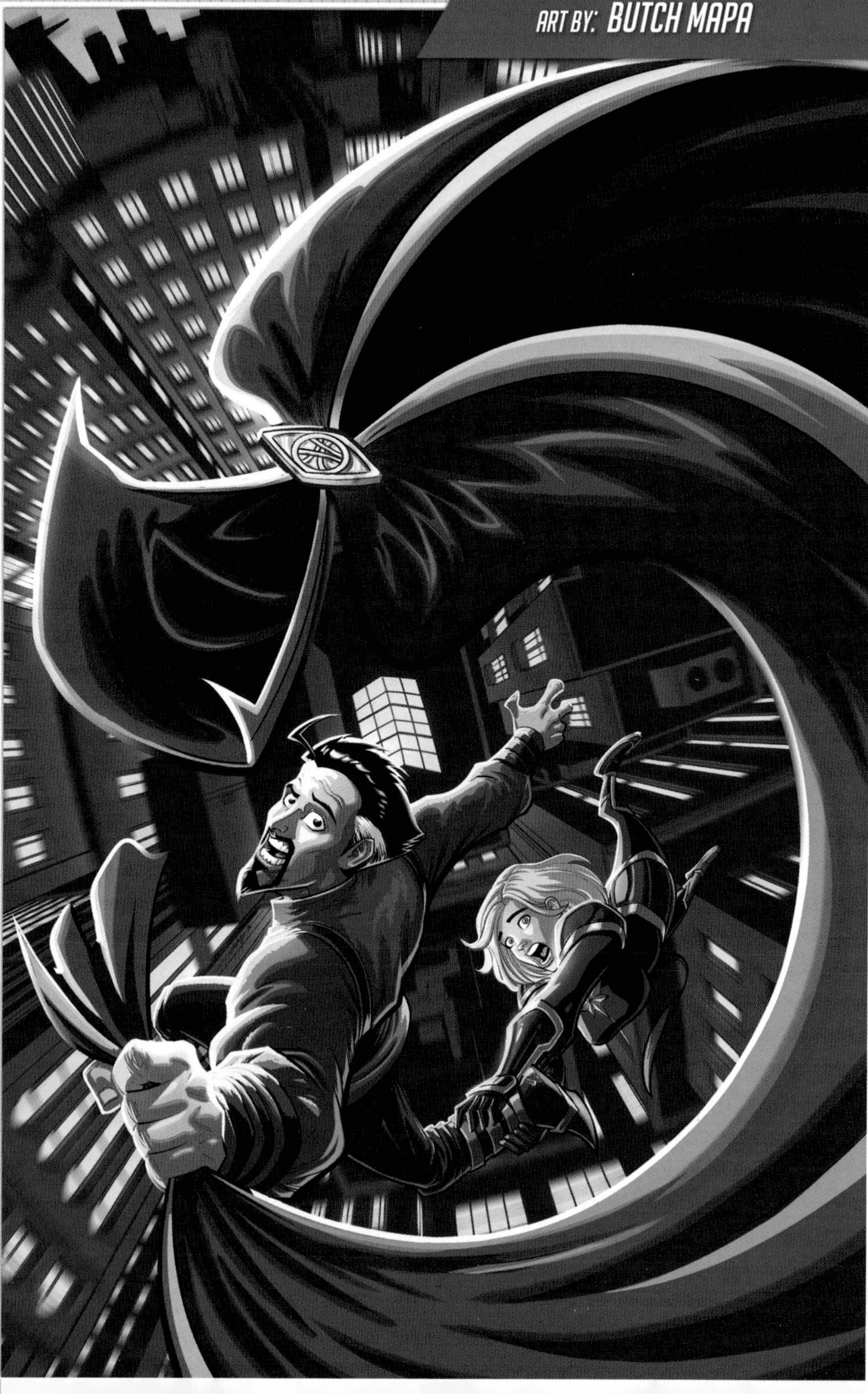

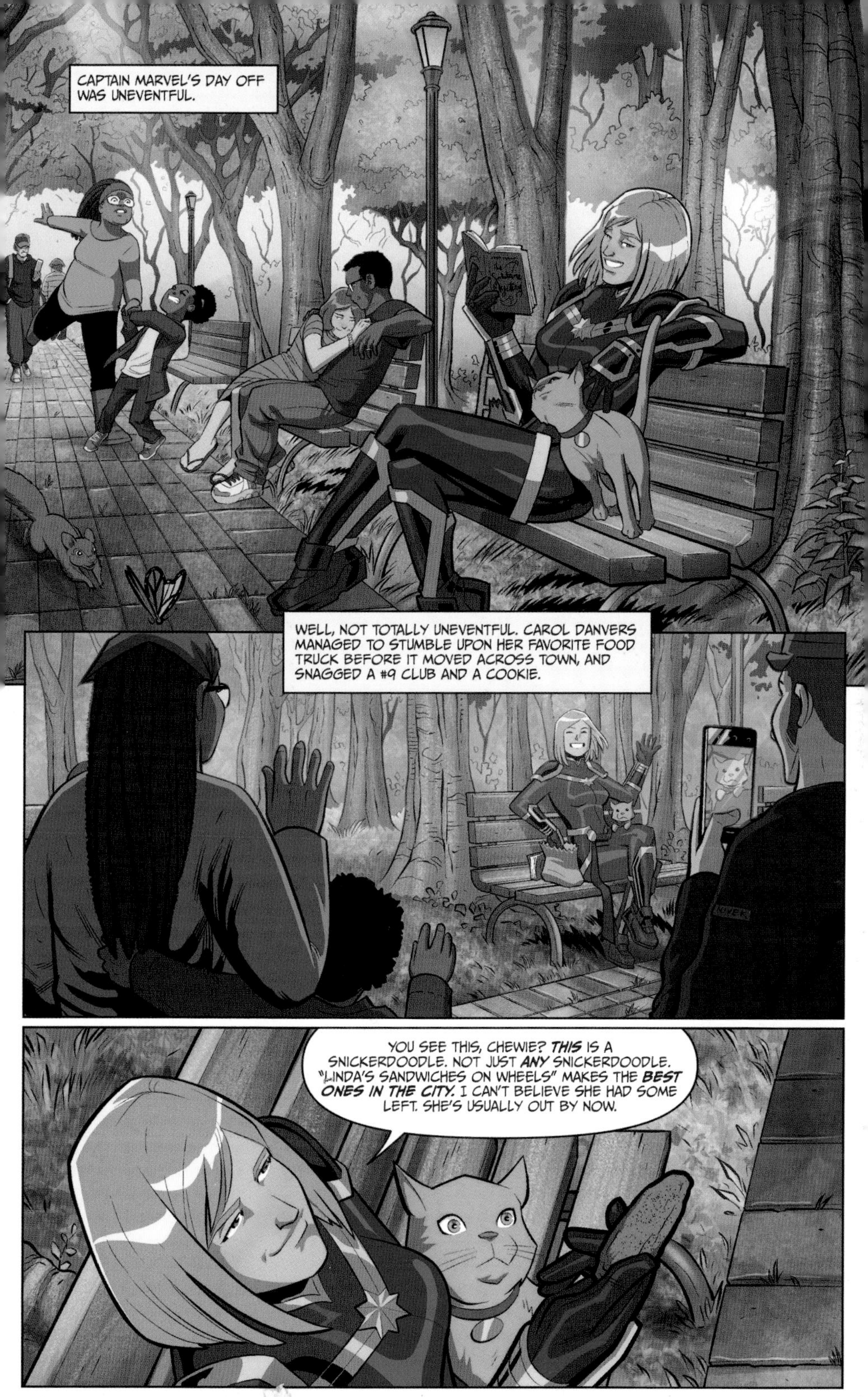
CAPTAIN MARVEL'S DAY OFF WAS UNEVENTFUL.
WELL, NOT TOTALLY UNEVENTFUL. CAROL DANVERS MANAGED TO STUMBLE UPON HER FAVORITE FOOD TRUCK BEFORE IT MOVED ACROSS TOWN, AND SNAGGED A #9 CLUB AND A COOKIE.
YOU SEE THIS, CHEWIE? ***THIS*** IS A SNICKERDOODLE. NOT JUST ***ANY*** SNICKERDOODLE. "LINDA'S SANDWICHES ON WHEELS" MAKES THE ***BEST ONES IN THE CITY.*** I CAN'T BELIEVE SHE HAD SOME LEFT. SHE'S USUALLY OUT BY NOW.

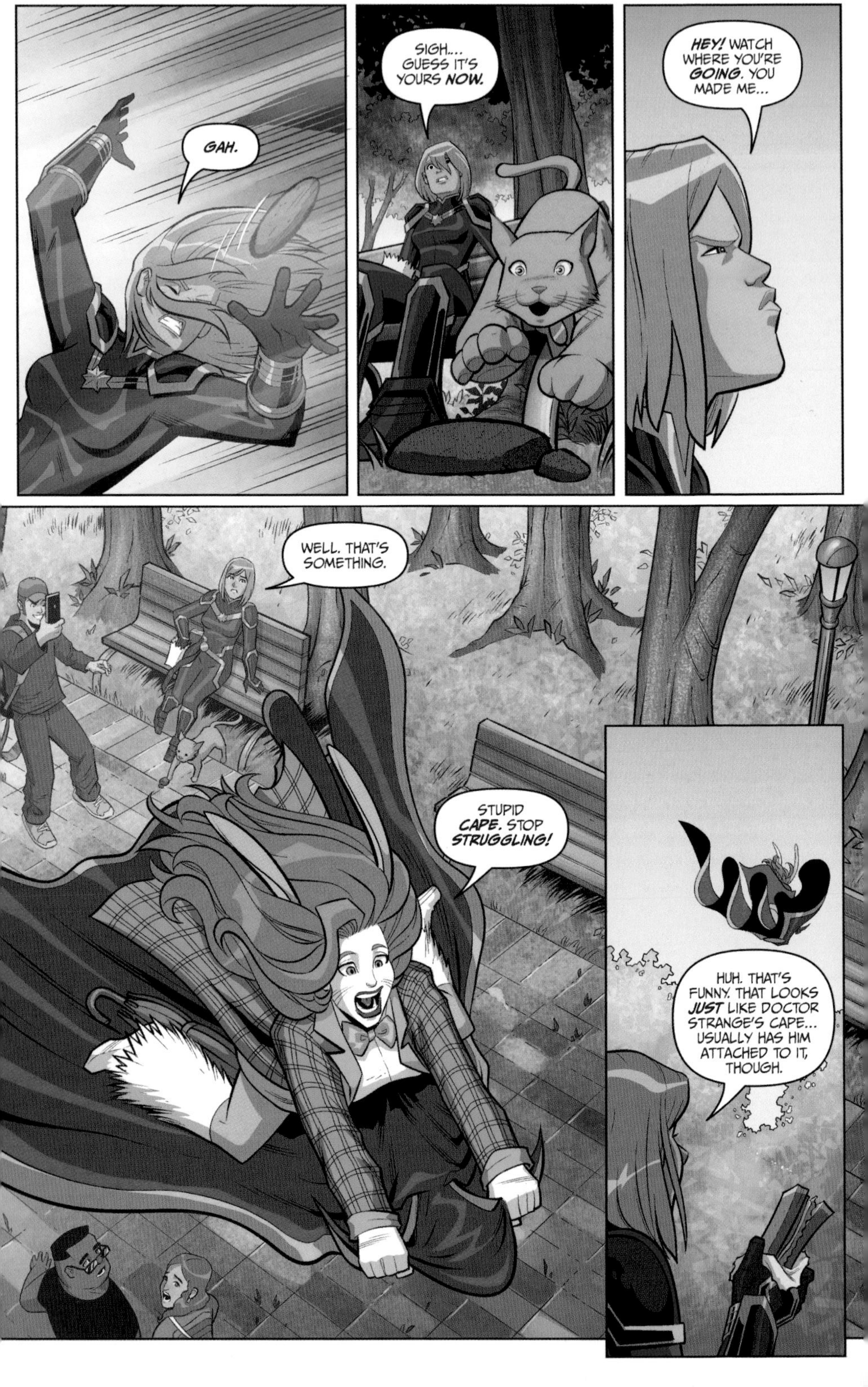
GAH.
SIGH... GUESS IT'S YOURS NOW.
HEY! WATCH WHERE YOU'RE GOING. YOU MADE ME...
WELL. THAT'S SOMETHING.
STUPID CAPE. STOP STRUGGLING!
HUH. THAT'S FUNNY. THAT LOOKS JUST LIKE DOCTOR STRANGE'S CAPE... USUALLY HAS HIM ATTACHED TO IT, THOUGH.

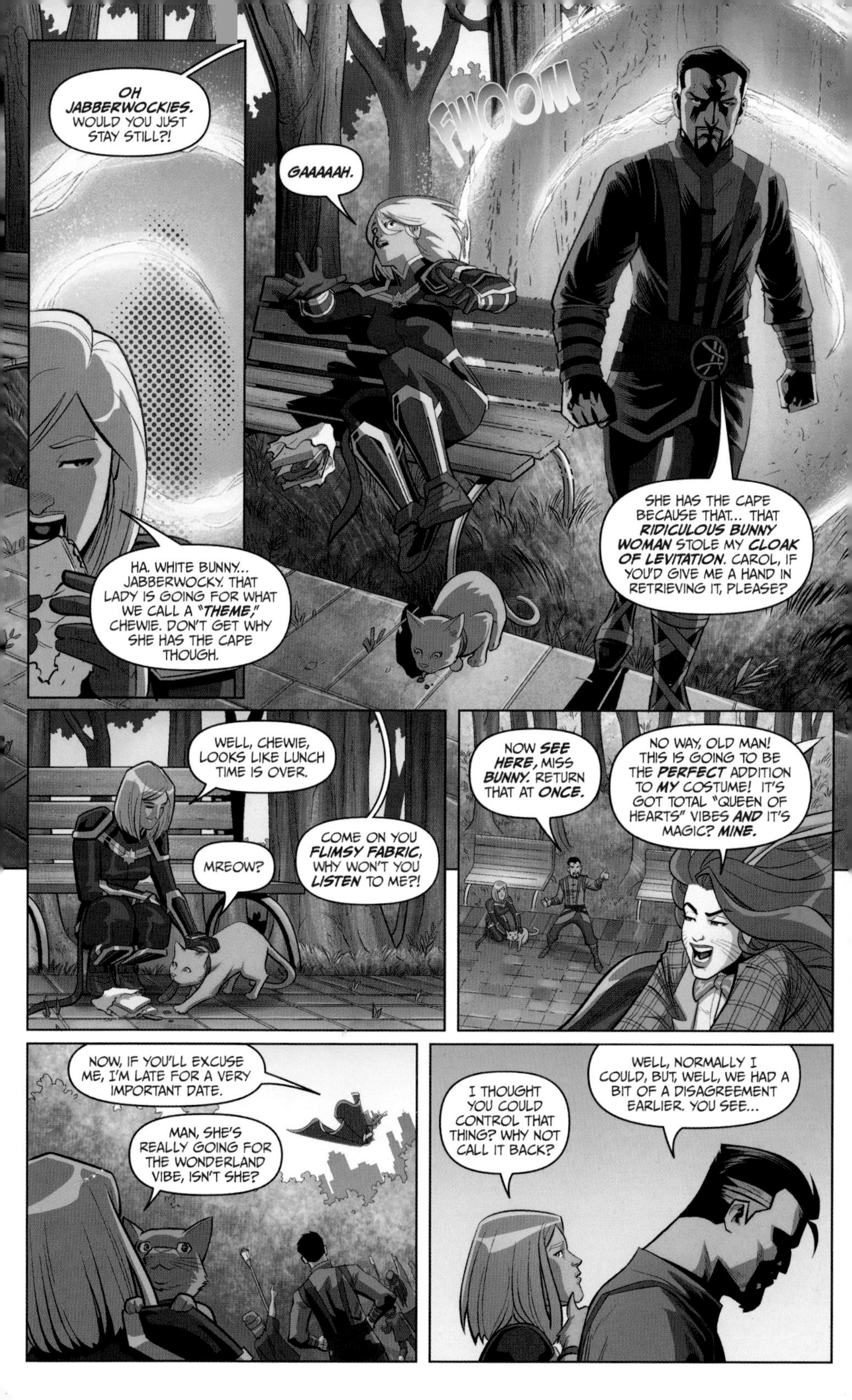
OH JABBERWOCKIES. WOULD YOU JUST STAY STILL?!
GAAAAAH.
FWOOM
SHE HAS THE CAPE BECAUSE THAT... THAT RIDICULOUS BUNNY WOMAN STOLE MY CLOAK OF LEVITATION. CAROL, IF YOU'D GIVE ME A HAND IN RETRIEVING IT, PLEASE?
HA. WHITE BUNNY... JABBERWOCKY. THAT LADY IS GOING FOR WHAT WE CALL A "THEME," CHEWIE. DON'T GET WHY SHE HAS THE CAPE THOUGH.
WELL, CHEWIE, LOOKS LIKE LUNCH TIME IS OVER.
MREOW?
COME ON YOU FLIMSY FABRIC, WHY WON'T YOU LISTEN TO ME?!
NOW SEE HERE, MISS BUNNY. RETURN THAT AT ONCE.
NO WAY, OLD MAN! THIS IS GOING TO BE THE PERFECT ADDITION TO MY COSTUME! IT'S GOT TOTAL "QUEEN OF HEARTS" VIBES AND IT'S MAGIC? MINE.
NOW, IF YOU'LL EXCUSE ME, I'M LATE FOR A VERY IMPORTANT DATE.
MAN, SHE'S REALLY GOING FOR THE WONDERLAND VIBE, ISN'T SHE?
I THOUGHT YOU COULD CONTROL THAT THING? WHY NOT CALL IT BACK?
WELL, NORMALLY I COULD, BUT, WELL, WE HAD A BIT OF A DISAGREEMENT EARLIER. YOU SEE...

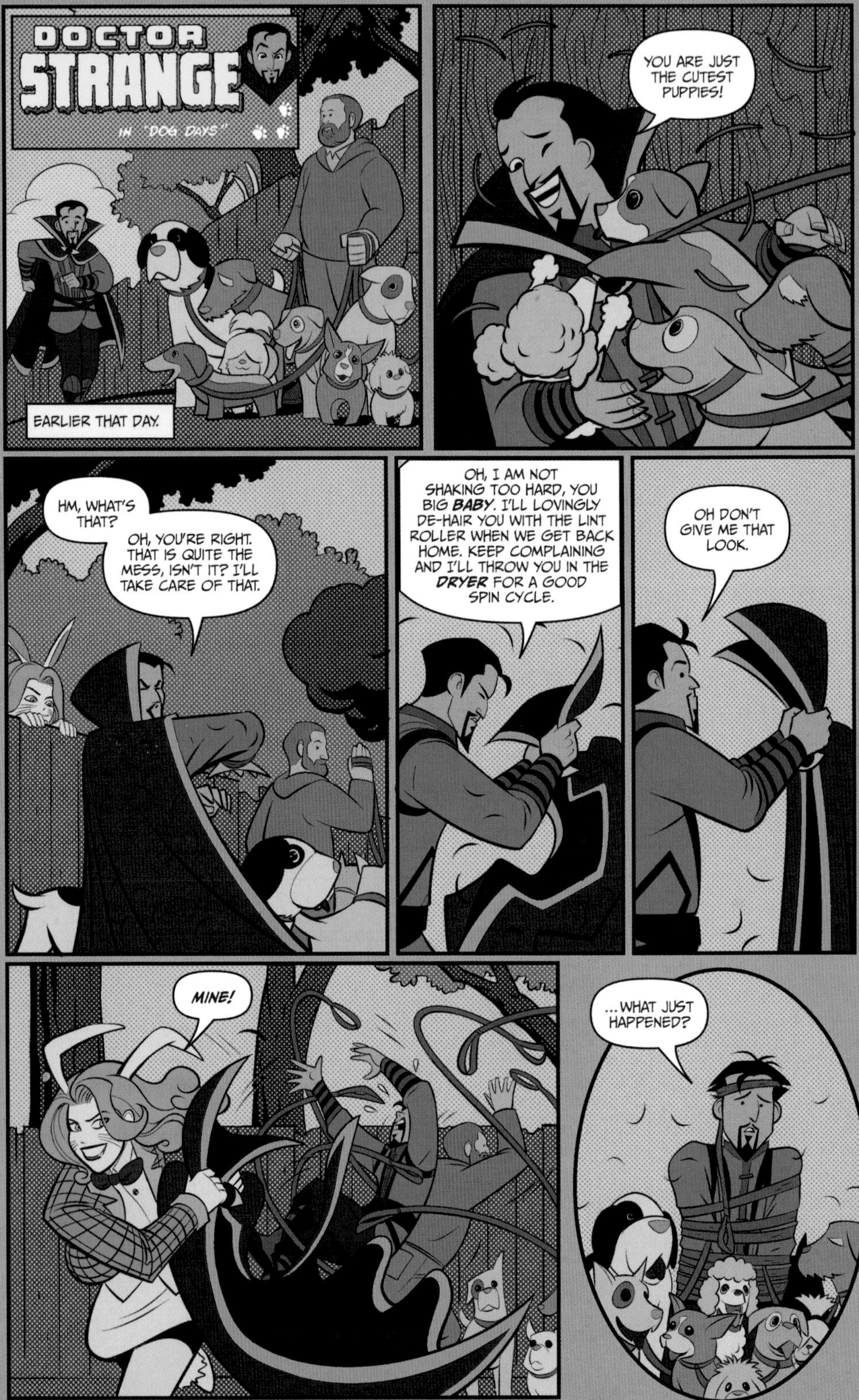
DOCTOR STRANGE
IN "DOG DAYS"
EARLIER THAT DAY.
YOU ARE JUST THE CUTEST PUPPIES!
HM, WHAT'S THAT?
OH, YOU'RE RIGHT. THAT IS QUITE THE MESS, ISN'T IT? I'LL TAKE CARE OF THAT.
OH, I AM NOT SHAKING TOO HARD, YOU BIG BABY. I'LL LOVINGLY DE-HAIR YOU WITH THE LINT ROLLER WHEN WE GET BACK HOME. KEEP COMPLAINING AND I'LL THROW YOU IN THE DRYER FOR A GOOD SPIN CYCLE.
OH DON'T GIVE ME THAT LOOK.
MINE!
...WHAT JUST HAPPENED?

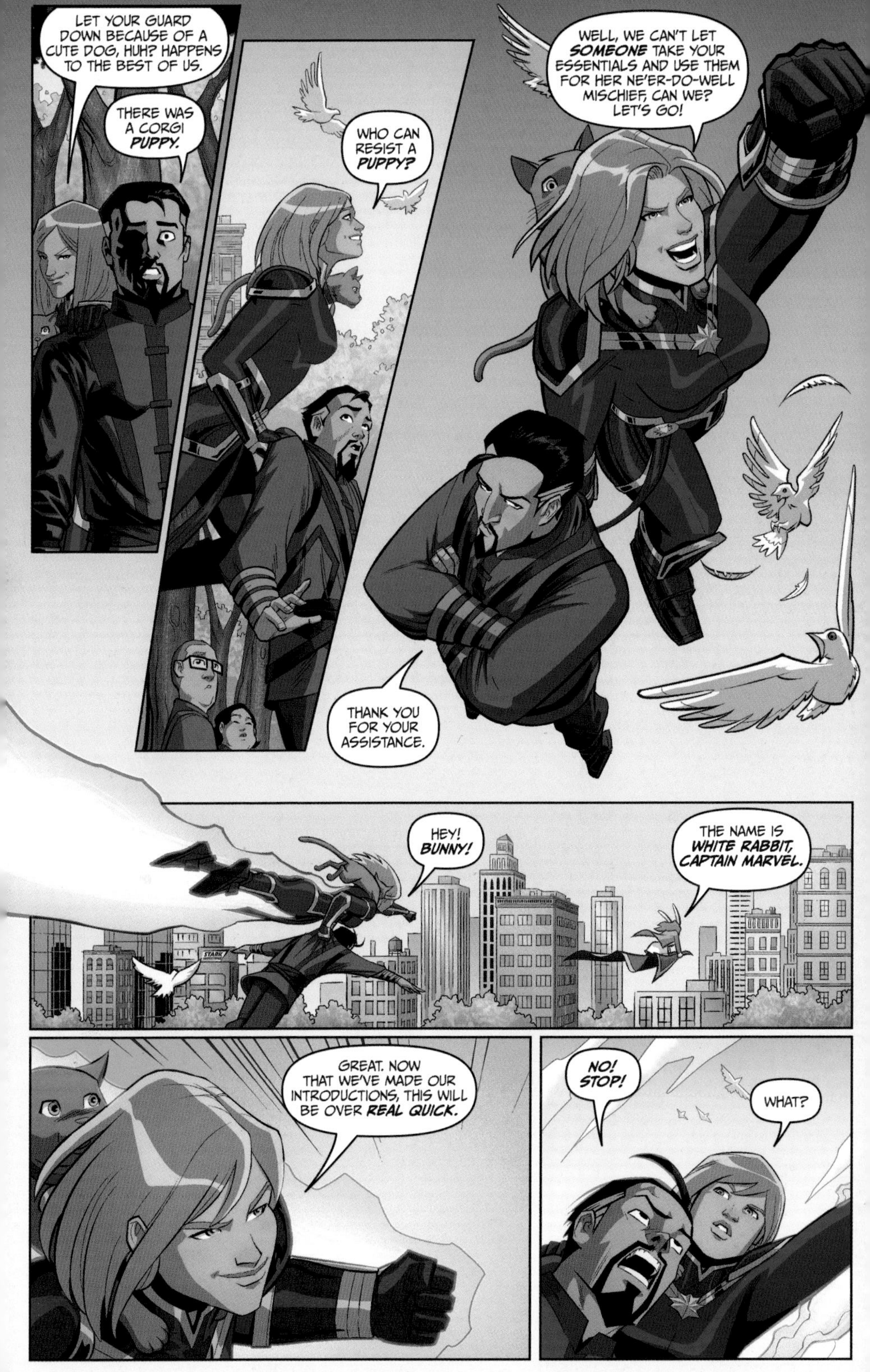
LET YOUR GUARD DOWN BECAUSE OF A CUTE DOG, HUH? HAPPENS TO THE BEST OF US.
THERE WAS A CORGI *PUPPY.*
WHO CAN RESIST A *PUPPY?*
WELL, WE CAN'T LET *SOMEONE* TAKE YOUR ESSENTIALS AND USE THEM FOR HER NE'ER-DO-WELL MISCHIEF, CAN WE? LET'S GO!
THANK YOU FOR YOUR ASSISTANCE.
HEY! *BUNNY!*
THE NAME IS *WHITE RABBIT, CAPTAIN MARVEL.*
STARK
GREAT. NOW THAT WE'VE MADE OUR INTRODUCTIONS, THIS WILL BE OVER *REAL QUICK.*
NO! STOP!
WHAT?

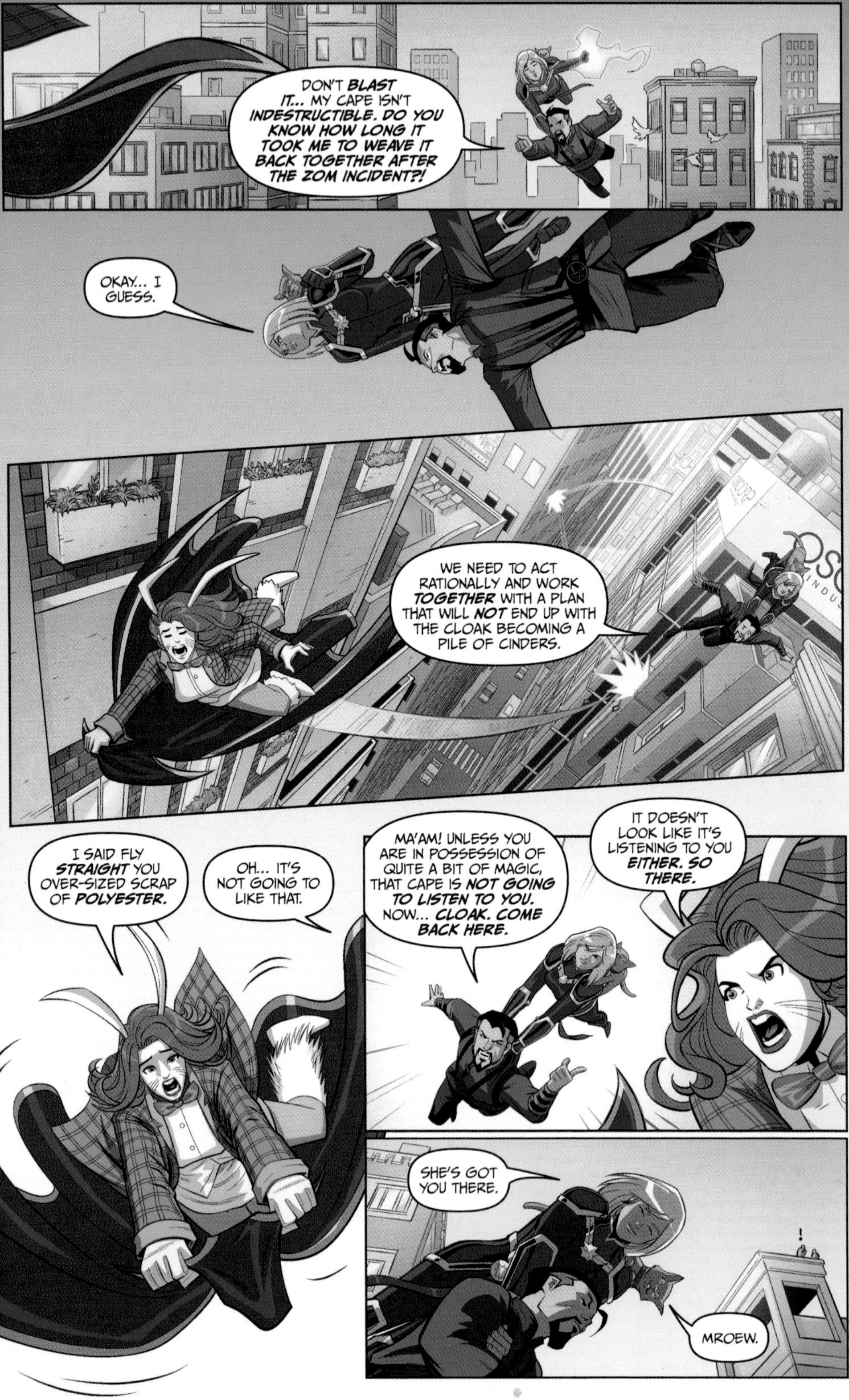
DON'T BLAST IT... MY CAPE ISN'T INDESTRUCTIBLE. DO YOU KNOW HOW LONG IT TOOK ME TO WEAVE IT BACK TOGETHER AFTER THE ZOM INCIDENT?!
OKAY... I GUESS.
WE NEED TO ACT RATIONALLY AND WORK TOGETHER WITH A PLAN THAT WILL NOT END UP WITH THE CLOAK BECOMING A PILE OF CINDERS.
I SAID FLY STRAIGHT YOU OVER-SIZED SCRAP OF POLYESTER.
OH... IT'S NOT GOING TO LIKE THAT.
MA'AM! UNLESS YOU ARE IN POSSESSION OF QUITE A BIT OF MAGIC, THAT CAPE IS NOT GOING TO LISTEN TO YOU. NOW... CLOAK. COME BACK HERE.
IT DOESN'T LOOK LIKE IT'S LISTENING TO YOU EITHER. SO THERE.
SHE'S GOT YOU THERE.
!
MROEW.

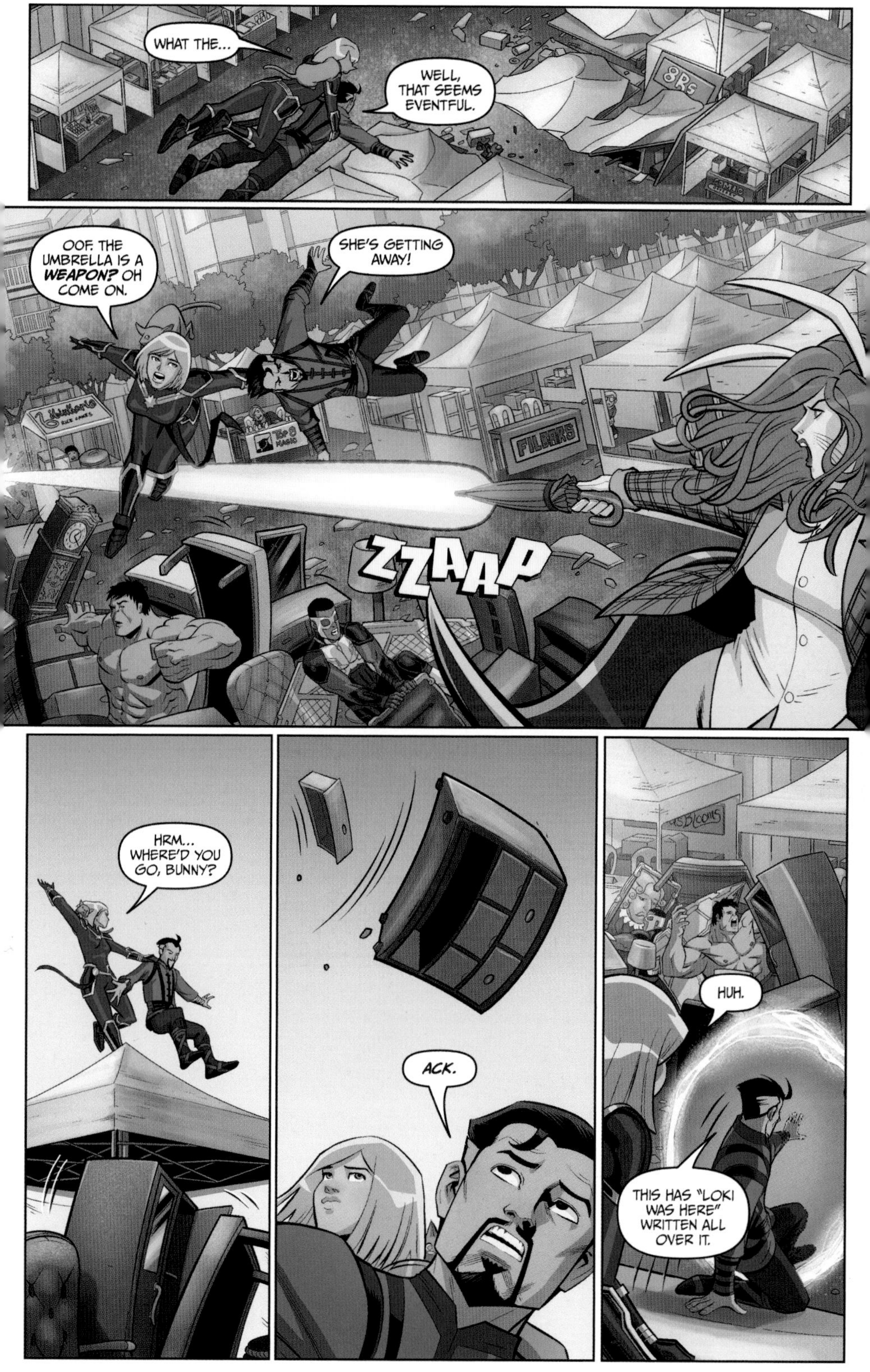
WHAT THE...
WELL, THAT SEEMS EVENTFUL.
OOF. THE UMBRELLA IS A WEAPON? OH COME ON.
SHE'S GETTING AWAY!
ZZAAAP
HRM... WHERE'D YOU GO, BUNNY?
ACK.
HUH.
THIS HAS "LOKI WAS HERE" WRITTEN ALL OVER IT.

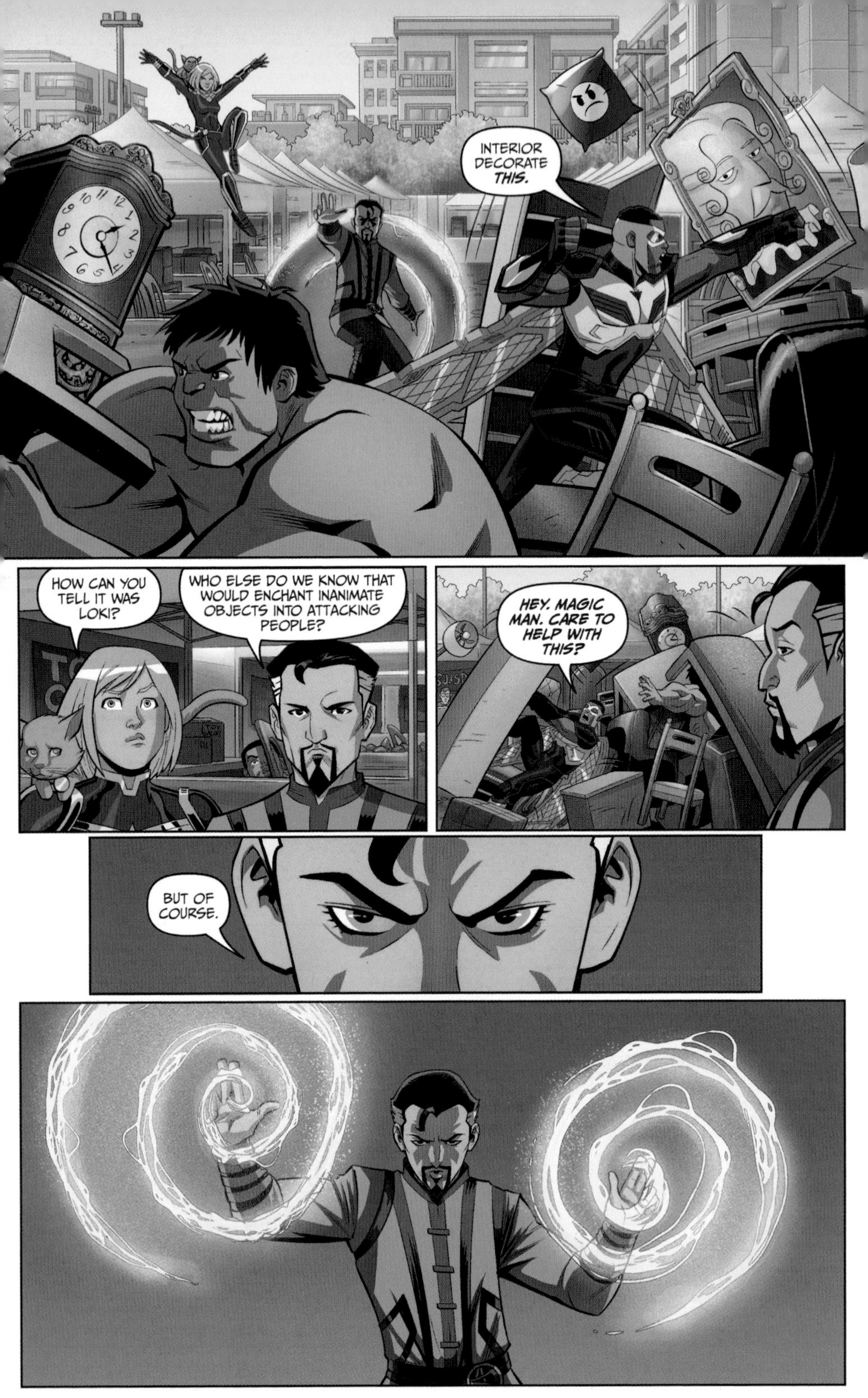
INTERIOR DECORATE THIS.
HOW CAN YOU TELL IT WAS LOKI?
WHO ELSE DO WE KNOW THAT WOULD ENCHANT INANIMATE OBJECTS INTO ATTACKING PEOPLE?
HEY. MAGIC MAN. CARE TO HELP WITH THIS?
BUT OF COURSE.

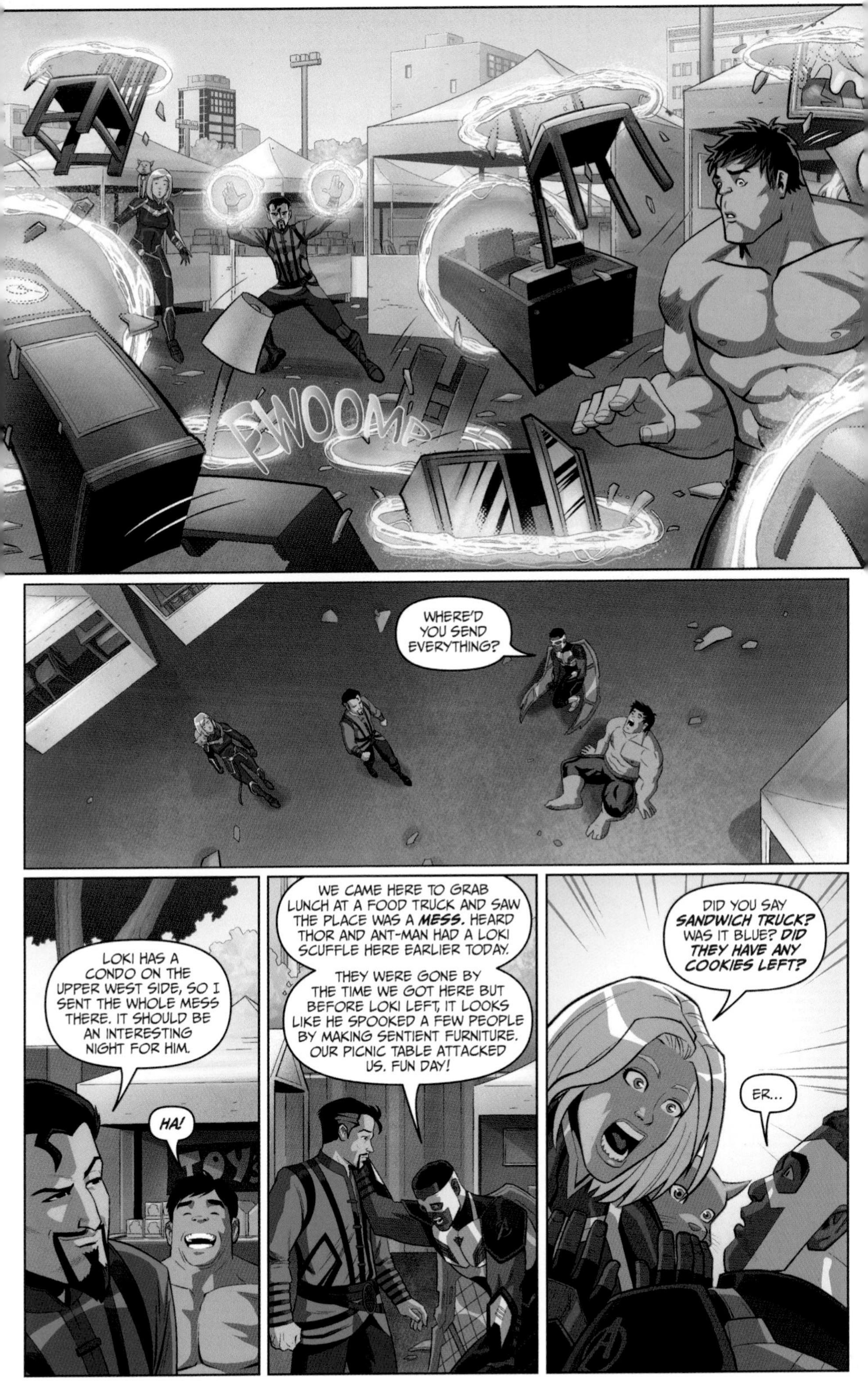
FWOOMP
WHERE'D YOU SEND EVERYTHING?
LOKI HAS A CONDO ON THE UPPER WEST SIDE, SO I SENT THE WHOLE MESS THERE. IT SHOULD BE AN INTERESTING NIGHT FOR HIM.
HA!
WE CAME HERE TO GRAB LUNCH AT A FOOD TRUCK AND SAW THE PLACE WAS A MESS. HEARD THOR AND ANT-MAN HAD A LOKI SCUFFLE HERE EARLIER TODAY.
THEY WERE GONE BY THE TIME WE GOT HERE BUT BEFORE LOKI LEFT, IT LOOKS LIKE HE SPOOKED A FEW PEOPLE BY MAKING SENTIENT FURNITURE. OUR PICNIC TABLE ATTACKED US. FUN DAY!
DID YOU SAY SANDWICH TRUCK? WAS IT BLUE? DID THEY HAVE ANY COOKIES LEFT?
ER...

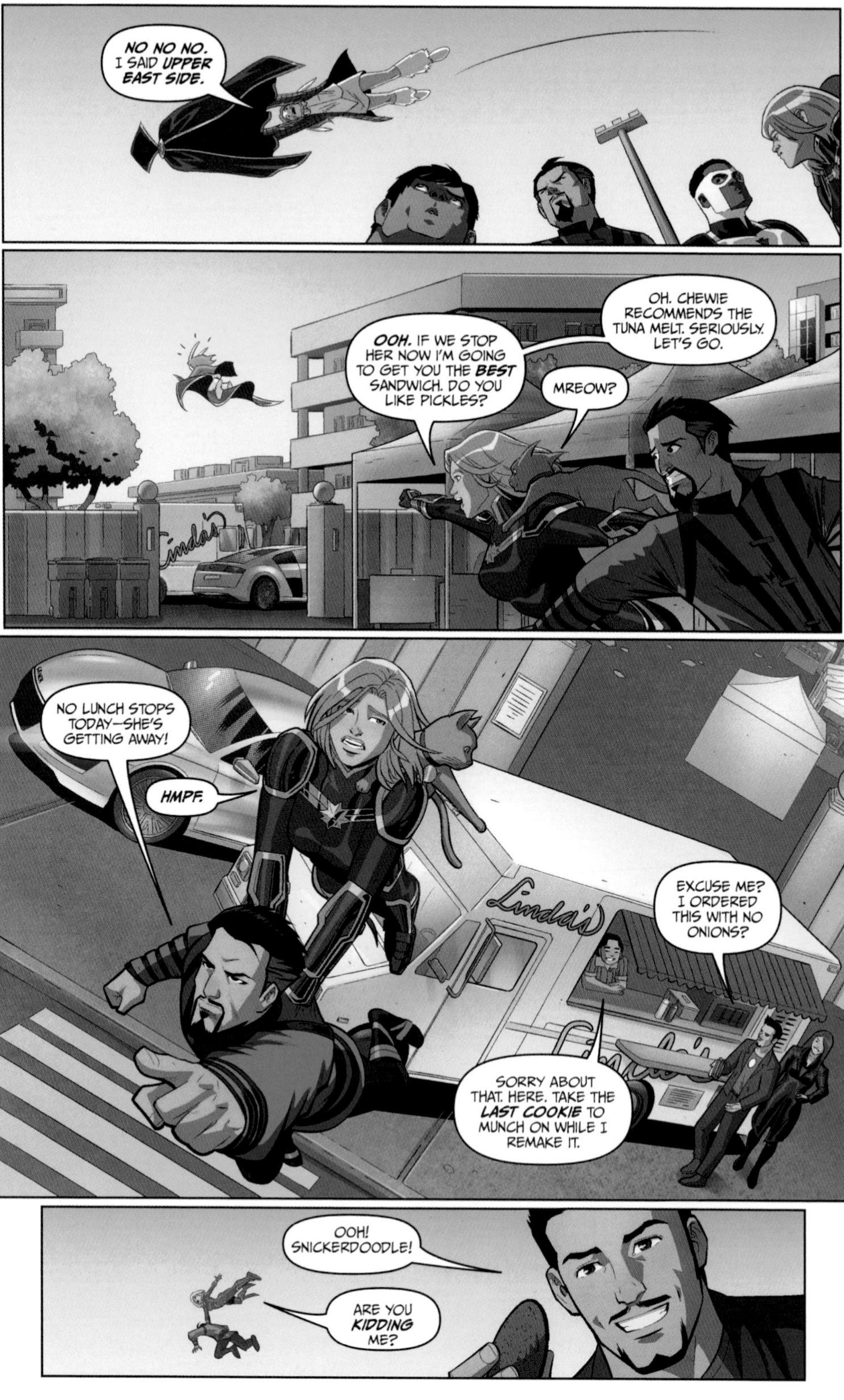
NO NO NO. I SAID UPPER EAST SIDE.
OOH. IF WE STOP HER NOW I'M GOING TO GET YOU THE BEST SANDWICH. DO YOU LIKE PICKLES?
OH. CHEWIE RECOMMENDS THE TUNA MELT. SERIOUSLY. LET'S GO.
MREOW?
Linda's
NO LUNCH STOPS TODAY—SHE'S GETTING AWAY!
HMPF.
EXCUSE ME? I ORDERED THIS WITH NO ONIONS?
SORRY ABOUT THAT. HERE. TAKE THE LAST COOKIE TO MUNCH ON WHILE I REMAKE IT.
OOH! SNICKERDOODLE!
ARE YOU KIDDING ME?

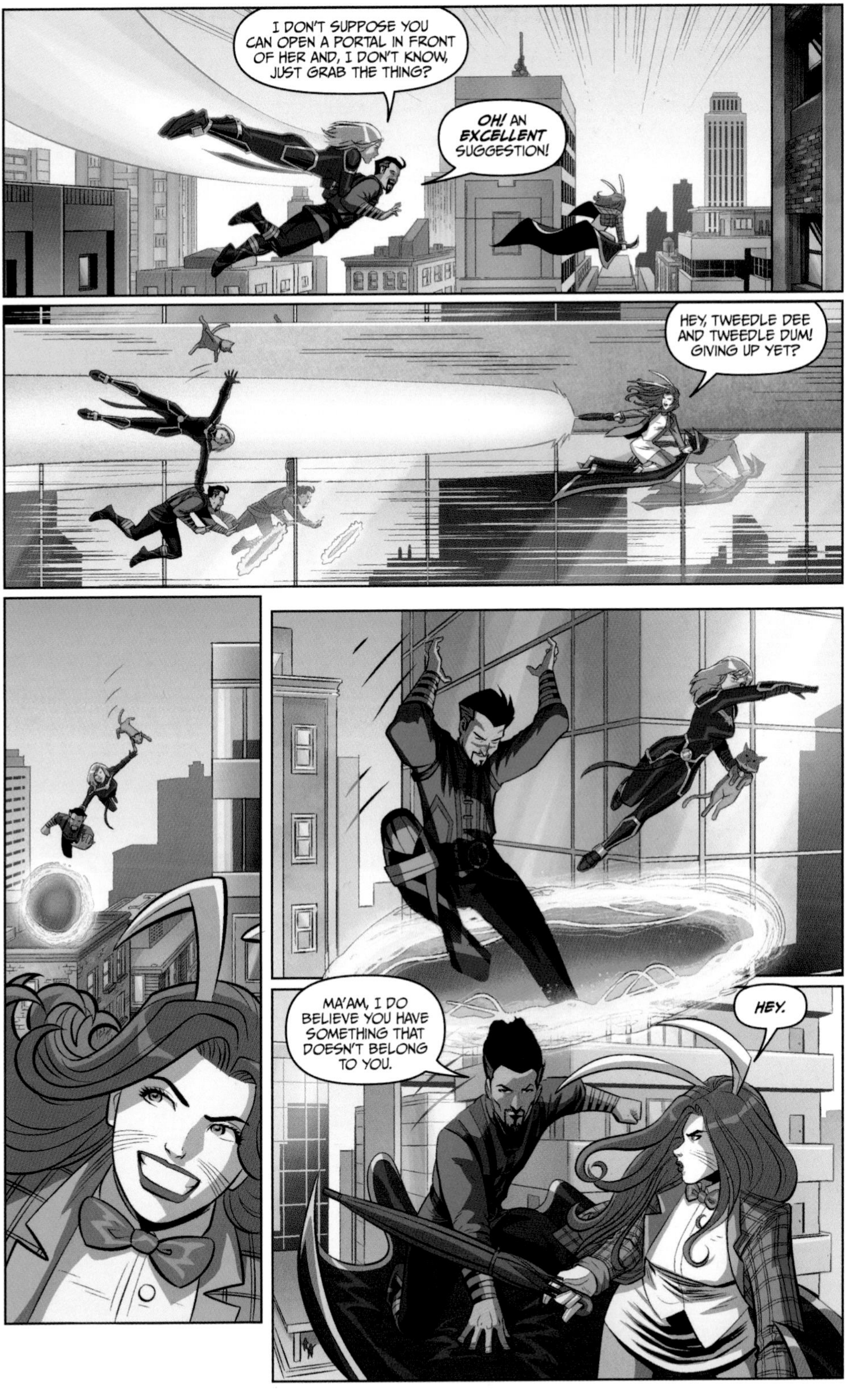
I DON'T SUPPOSE YOU CAN OPEN A PORTAL IN FRONT OF HER AND, I DON'T KNOW, JUST GRAB THE THING?
OH! AN EXCELLENT SUGGESTION!
HEY, TWEEDLE DEE AND TWEEDLE DUM! GIVING UP YET?
MA'AM, I DO BELIEVE YOU HAVE SOMETHING THAT DOESN'T BELONG TO YOU.
HEY.

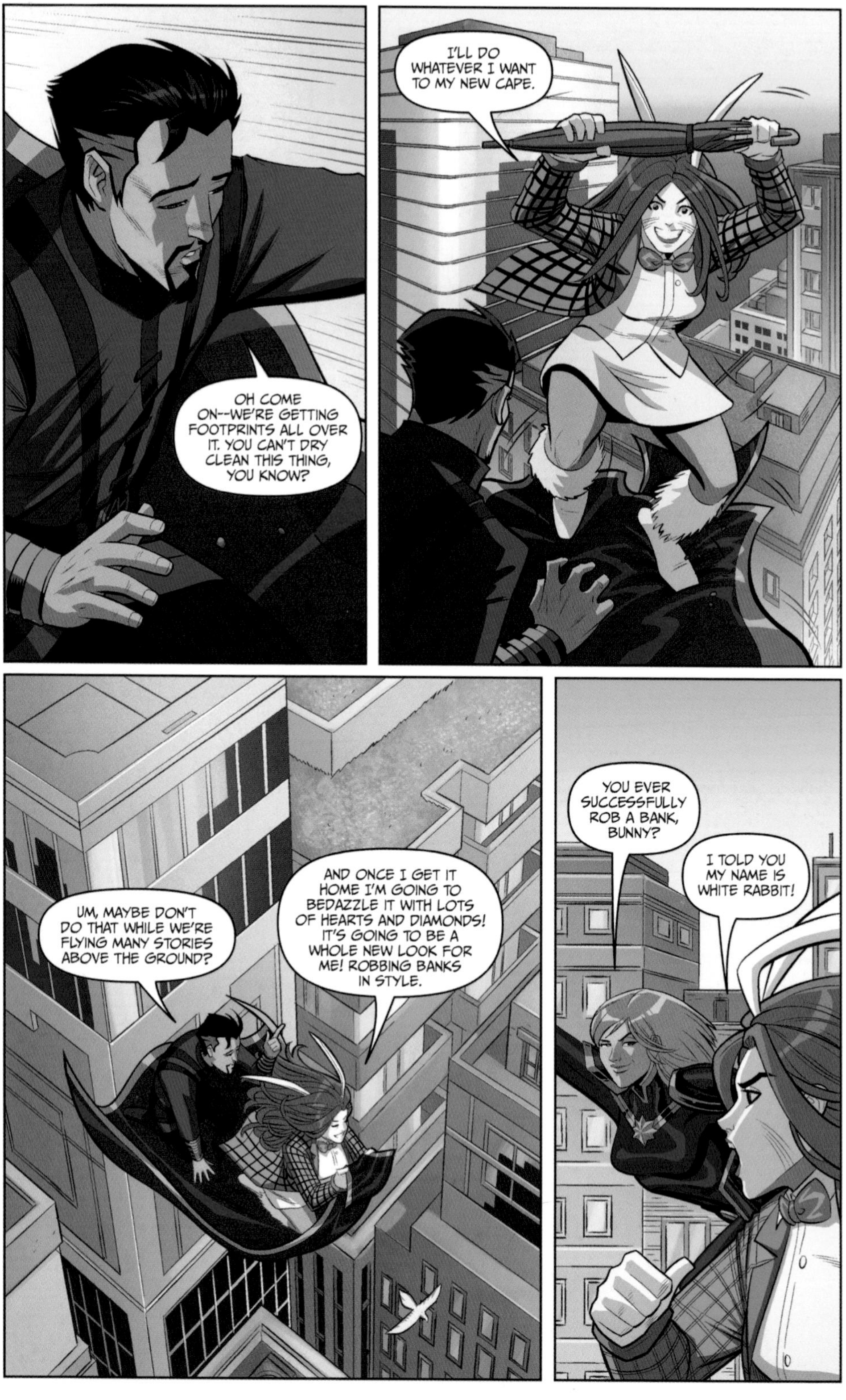
I'LL DO WHATEVER I WANT TO MY NEW CAPE.
OH COME ON--WE'RE GETTING FOOTPRINTS ALL OVER IT. YOU CAN'T DRY CLEAN THIS THING, YOU KNOW?
AND ONCE I GET IT HOME I'M GOING TO BEDAZZLE IT WITH LOTS OF HEARTS AND DIAMONDS! IT'S GOING TO BE A WHOLE NEW LOOK FOR ME! ROBBING BANKS IN STYLE.
UM, MAYBE DON'T DO THAT WHILE WE'RE FLYING MANY STORIES ABOVE THE GROUND?
YOU EVER SUCCESSFULLY ROB A BANK, BUNNY?
I TOLD YOU MY NAME IS WHITE RABBIT!

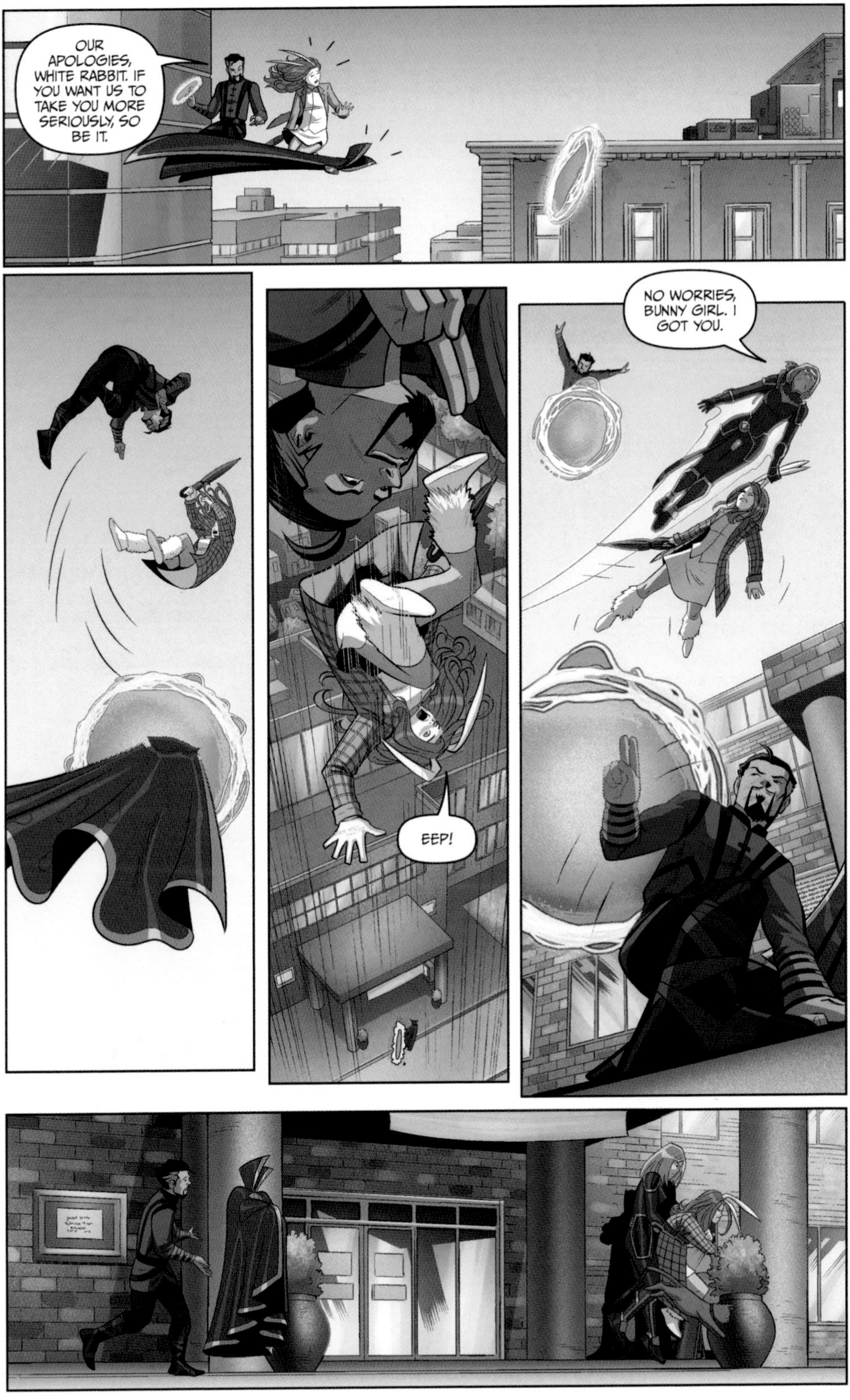
OUR APOLOGIES, WHITE RABBIT. IF YOU WANT US TO TAKE YOU MORE SERIOUSLY, SO BE IT.
EEP!
NO WORRIES, BUNNY GIRL. I GOT YOU.

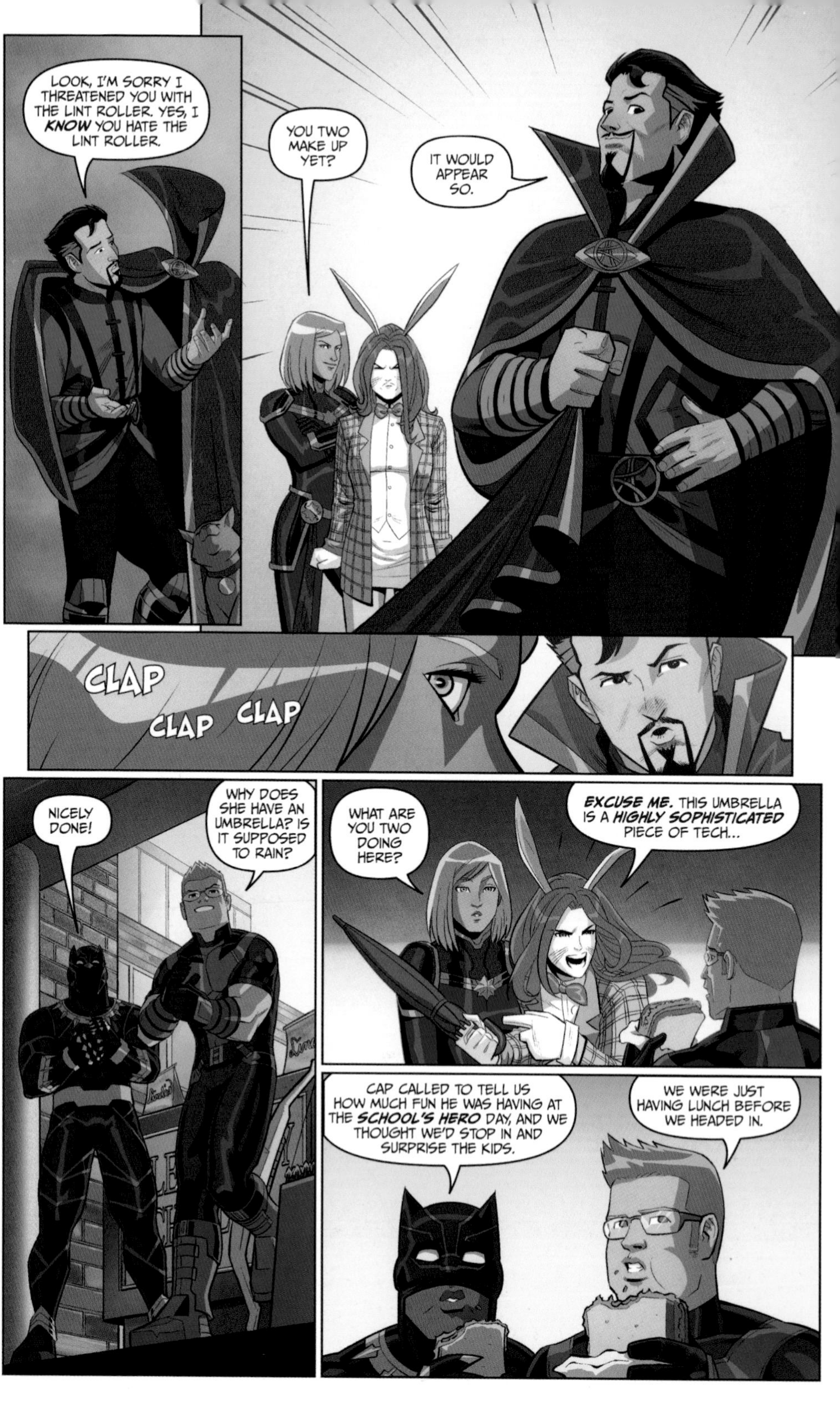
LOOK, I'M SORRY I THREATENED YOU WITH THE LINT ROLLER. YES, I KNOW YOU HATE THE LINT ROLLER.
YOU TWO MAKE UP YET?
IT WOULD APPEAR SO.
CLAP
CLAP CLAP
NICELY DONE!
WHY DOES SHE HAVE AN UMBRELLA? IS IT SUPPOSED TO RAIN?
WHAT ARE YOU TWO DOING HERE?
EXCUSE ME. THIS UMBRELLA IS A HIGHLY SOPHISTICATED PIECE OF TECH...
CAP CALLED TO TELL US HOW MUCH FUN HE WAS HAVING AT THE SCHOOL'S HERO DAY, AND WE THOUGHT WE'D STOP IN AND SURPRISE THE KIDS.
WE WERE JUST HAVING LUNCH BEFORE WE HEADED IN.

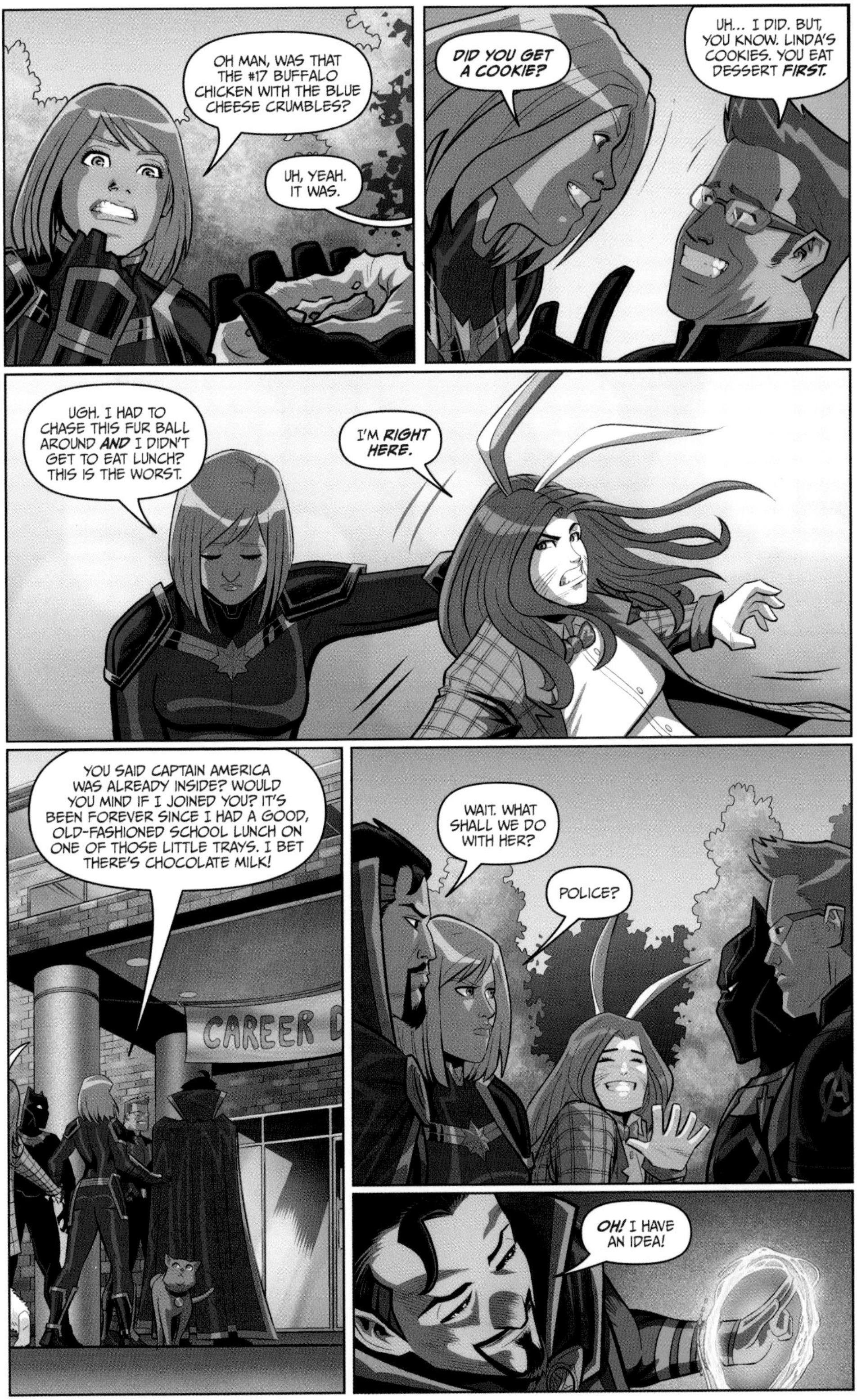
OH MAN, WAS THAT THE #17 BUFFALO CHICKEN WITH THE BLUE CHEESE CRUMBLES?
UH, YEAH. IT WAS.
DID YOU GET A COOKIE?
UH... I DID. BUT, YOU KNOW. LINDA'S COOKIES. YOU EAT DESSERT FIRST.
UGH. I HAD TO CHASE THIS FUR BALL AROUND AND I DIDN'T GET TO EAT LUNCH? THIS IS THE WORST.
I'M RIGHT HERE.
YOU SAID CAPTAIN AMERICA WAS ALREADY INSIDE? WOULD YOU MIND IF I JOINED YOU? IT'S BEEN FOREVER SINCE I HAD A GOOD, OLD-FASHIONED SCHOOL LUNCH ON ONE OF THOSE LITTLE TRAYS. I BET THERE'S CHOCOLATE MILK!
CAREER D
WAIT. WHAT SHALL WE DO WITH HER?
POLICE?
OH! I HAVE AN IDEA!

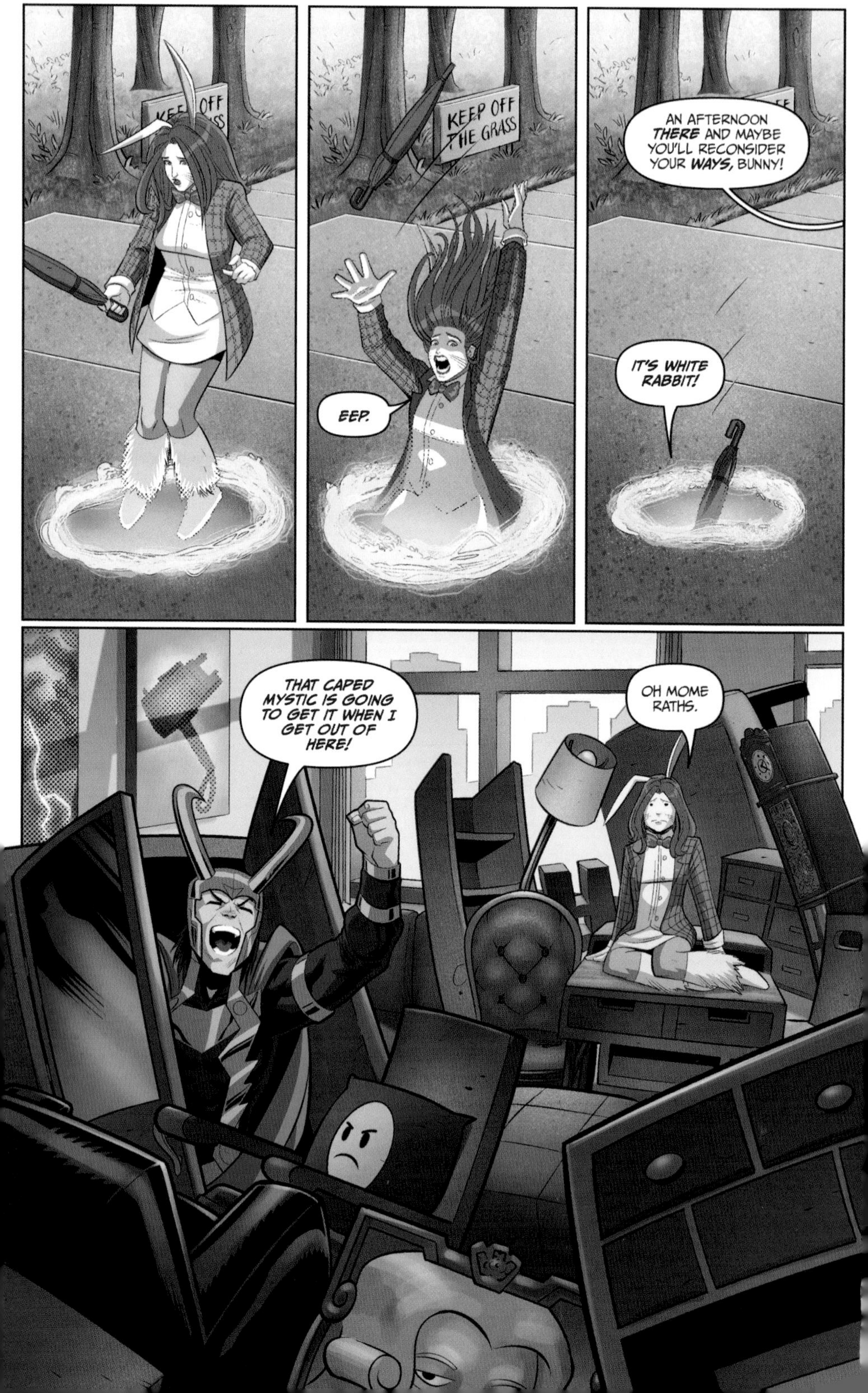
KEEP OFF THE GRASS
EEP.
AN AFTERNOON THERE AND MAYBE YOU'LL RECONSIDER YOUR WAYS, BUNNY!
IT'S WHITE RABBIT!
THAT CAPED MYSTIC IS GOING TO GET IT WHEN I GET OUT OF HERE!
OH MOME RATHS.

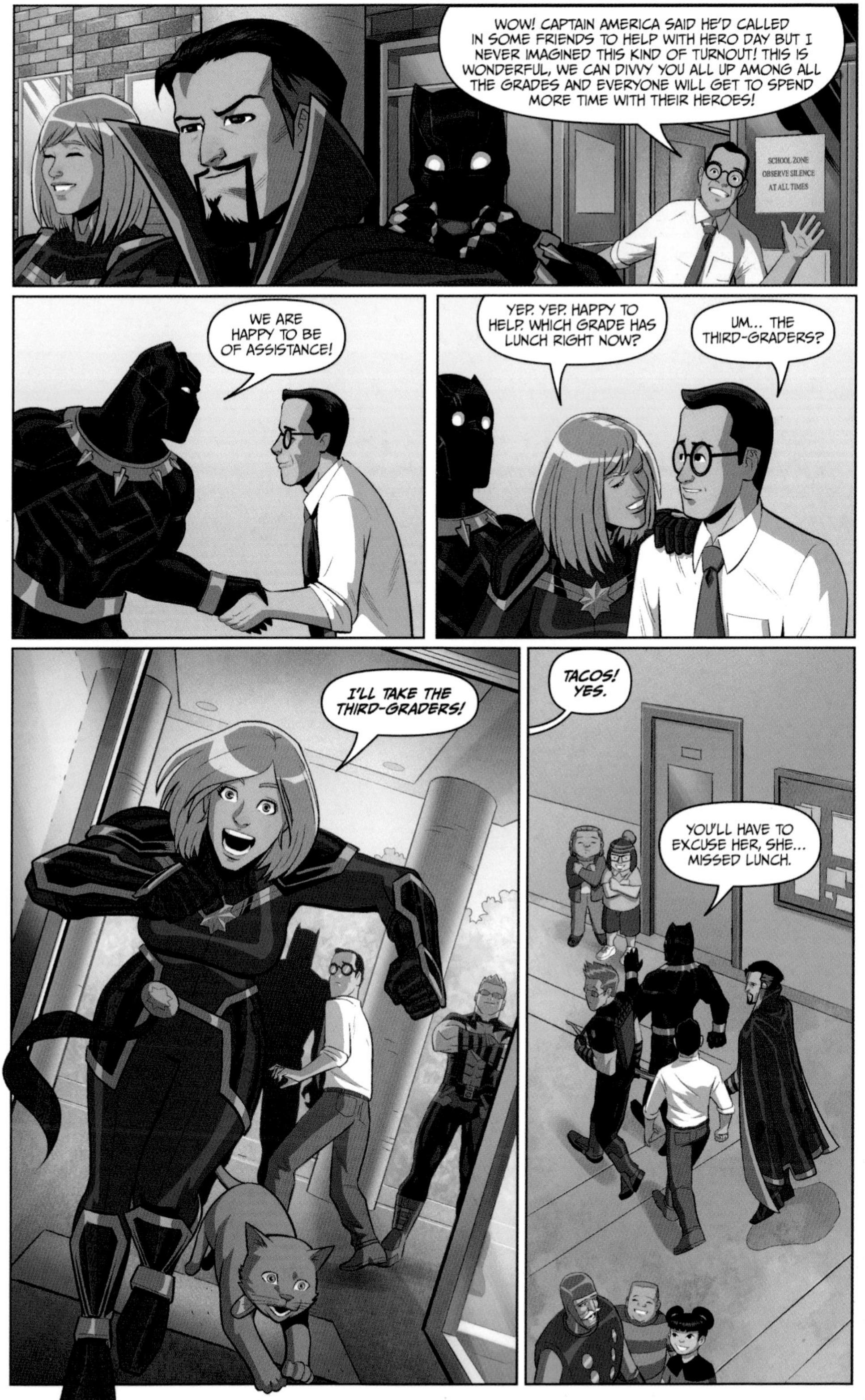
WOW! CAPTAIN AMERICA SAID HE'D CALLED IN SOME FRIENDS TO HELP WITH HERO DAY BUT I NEVER IMAGINED THIS KIND OF TURNOUT! THIS IS WONDERFUL, WE CAN DIVVY YOU ALL UP AMONG ALL THE GRADES AND EVERYONE WILL GET TO SPEND MORE TIME WITH THEIR HEROES!
SCHOOL ZONE OBSERVE SILENCE AT ALL TIMES
WE ARE HAPPY TO BE OF ASSISTANCE!
YEP. YEP. HAPPY TO HELP. WHICH GRADE HAS LUNCH RIGHT NOW?
UM... THE THIRD-GRADERS?
I'LL TAKE THE THIRD-GRADERS!
TACOS! YES.
YOU'LL HAVE TO EXCUSE HER, SHE... MISSED LUNCH.

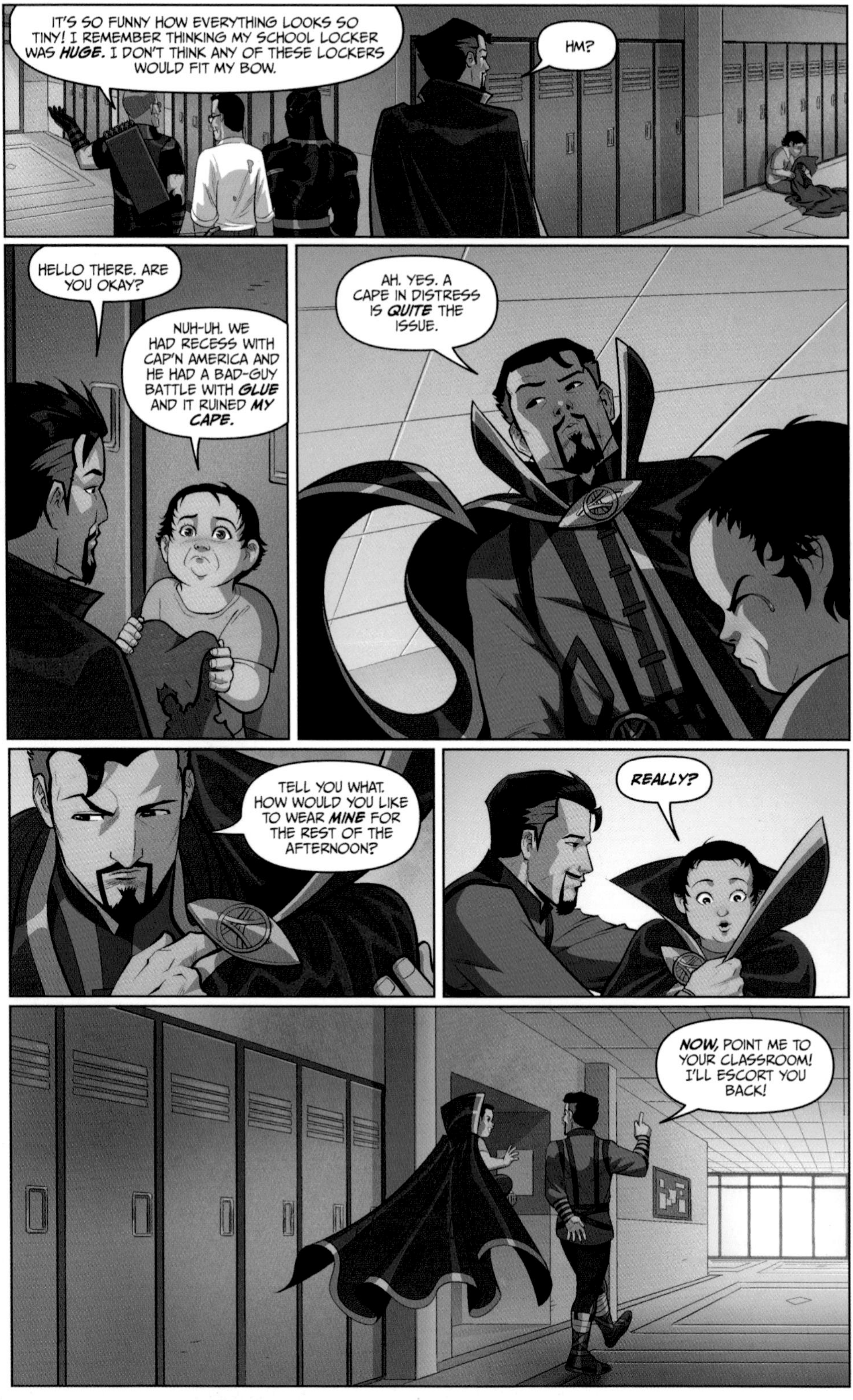

IT'S SO FUNNY HOW EVERYTHING LOOKS SO TINY! I REMEMBER THINKING MY SCHOOL LOCKER WAS HUGE. I DON'T THINK ANY OF THESE LOCKERS WOULD FIT MY BOW.
HM?
HELLO THERE. ARE YOU OKAY?
NUH-UH. WE HAD RECESS WITH CAP'N AMERICA AND HE HAD A BAD-GUY BATTLE WITH GLUE AND IT RUINED MY CAPE.
AH. YES. A CAPE IN DISTRESS IS QUITE THE ISSUE.
TELL YOU WHAT. HOW WOULD YOU LIKE TO WEAR MINE FOR THE REST OF THE AFTERNOON?
REALLY?
NOW, POINT ME TO YOUR CLASSROOM! I'LL ESCORT YOU BACK!

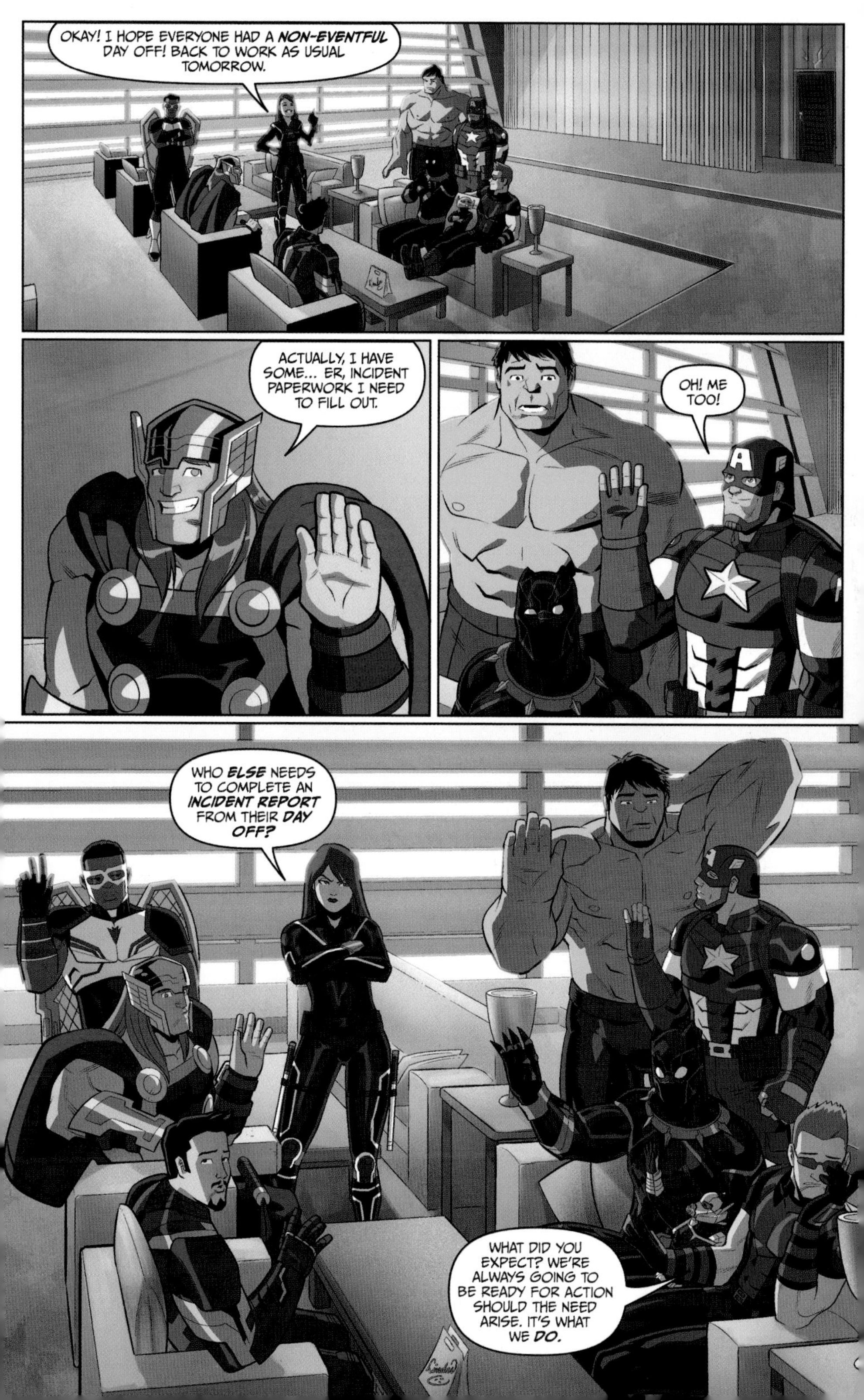
OKAY! I HOPE EVERYONE HAD A NON-EVENTFUL DAY OFF! BACK TO WORK AS USUAL TOMORROW.
ACTUALLY, I HAVE SOME... ER, INCIDENT PAPERWORK I NEED TO FILL OUT.
OH! ME TOO!
WHO ELSE NEEDS TO COMPLETE AN INCIDENT REPORT FROM THEIR DAY OFF?
WHAT DID YOU EXPECT? WE'RE ALWAYS GOING TO BE READY FOR ACTION SHOULD THE NEED ARISE. IT'S WHAT WE DO.

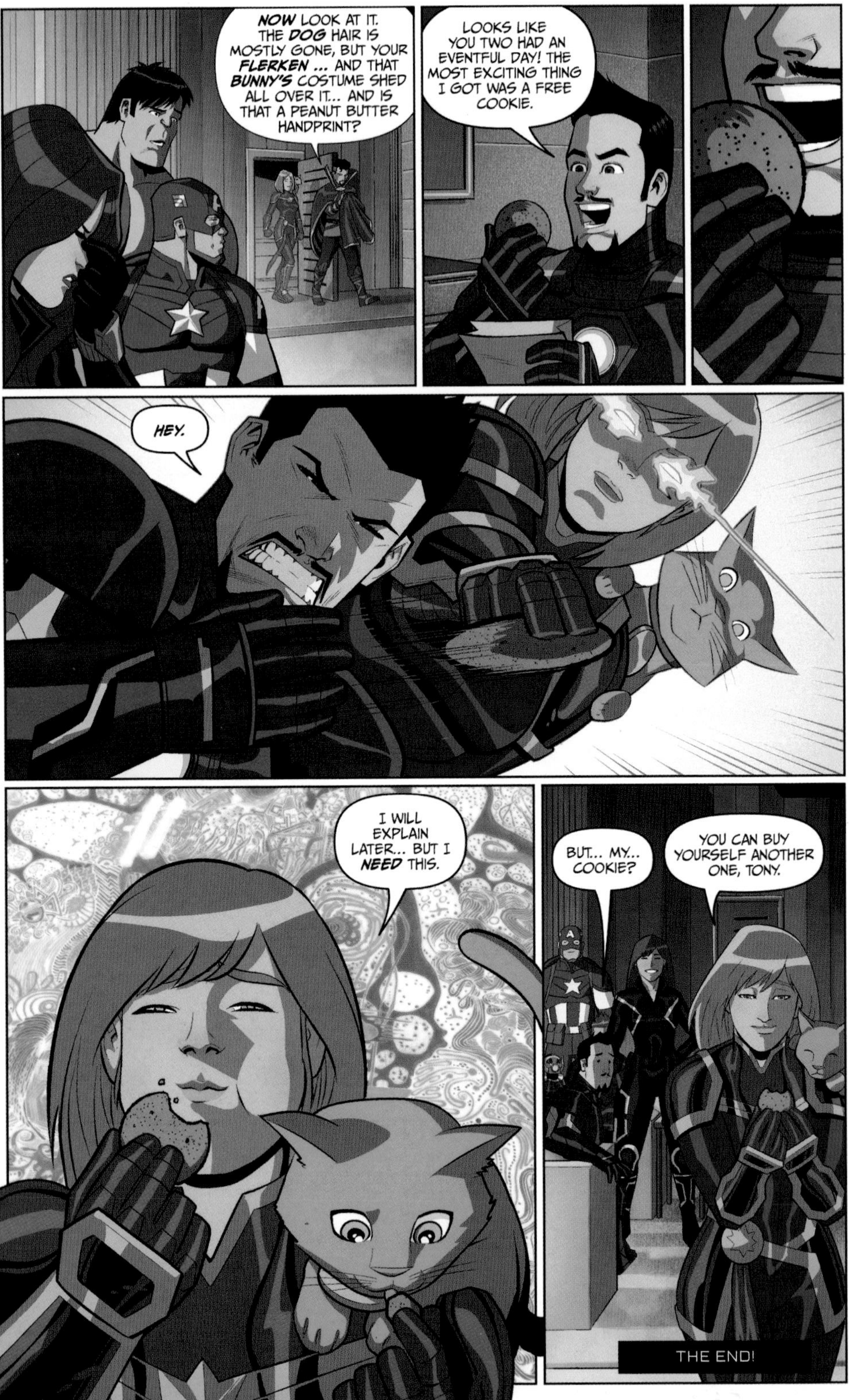
NOW LOOK AT IT. THE DOG HAIR IS MOSTLY GONE, BUT YOUR FLERKEN ... AND THAT BUNNY'S COSTUME SHED ALL OVER IT... AND IS THAT A PEANUT BUTTER HANDPRINT?
LOOKS LIKE YOU TWO HAD AN EVENTFUL DAY! THE MOST EXCITING THING I GOT WAS A FREE COOKIE.
HEY.
I WILL EXPLAIN LATER... BUT I NEED THIS.
BUT... MY... COOKIE?
YOU CAN BUY YOURSELF ANOTHER ONE, TONY.
THE END!

ART BY: RUAIRI COLEMAN
COLORS BY: BRACARDI CURRY

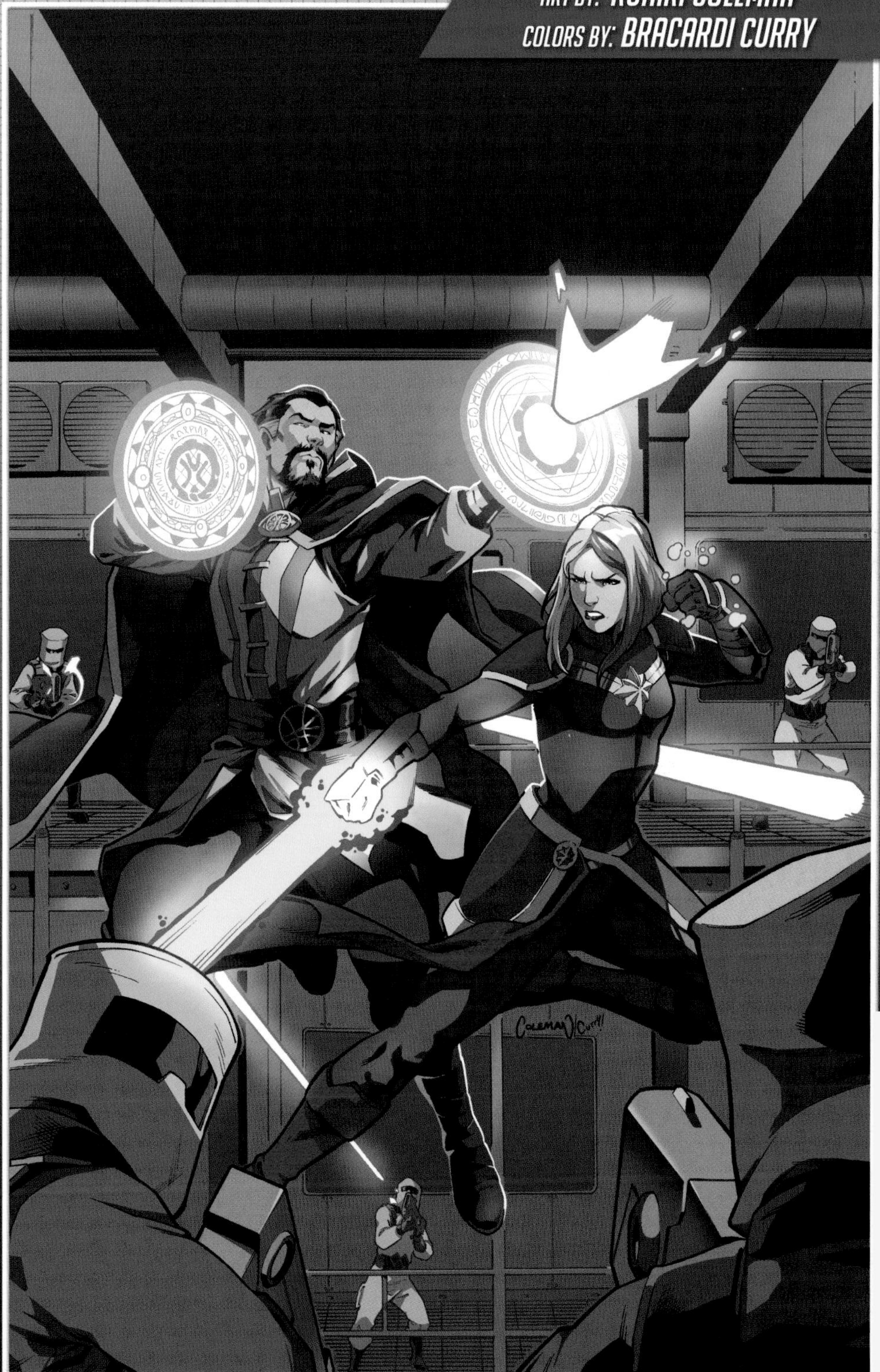

ANT-MAN

HELP ANT-MAN FIND HIS ANTS!

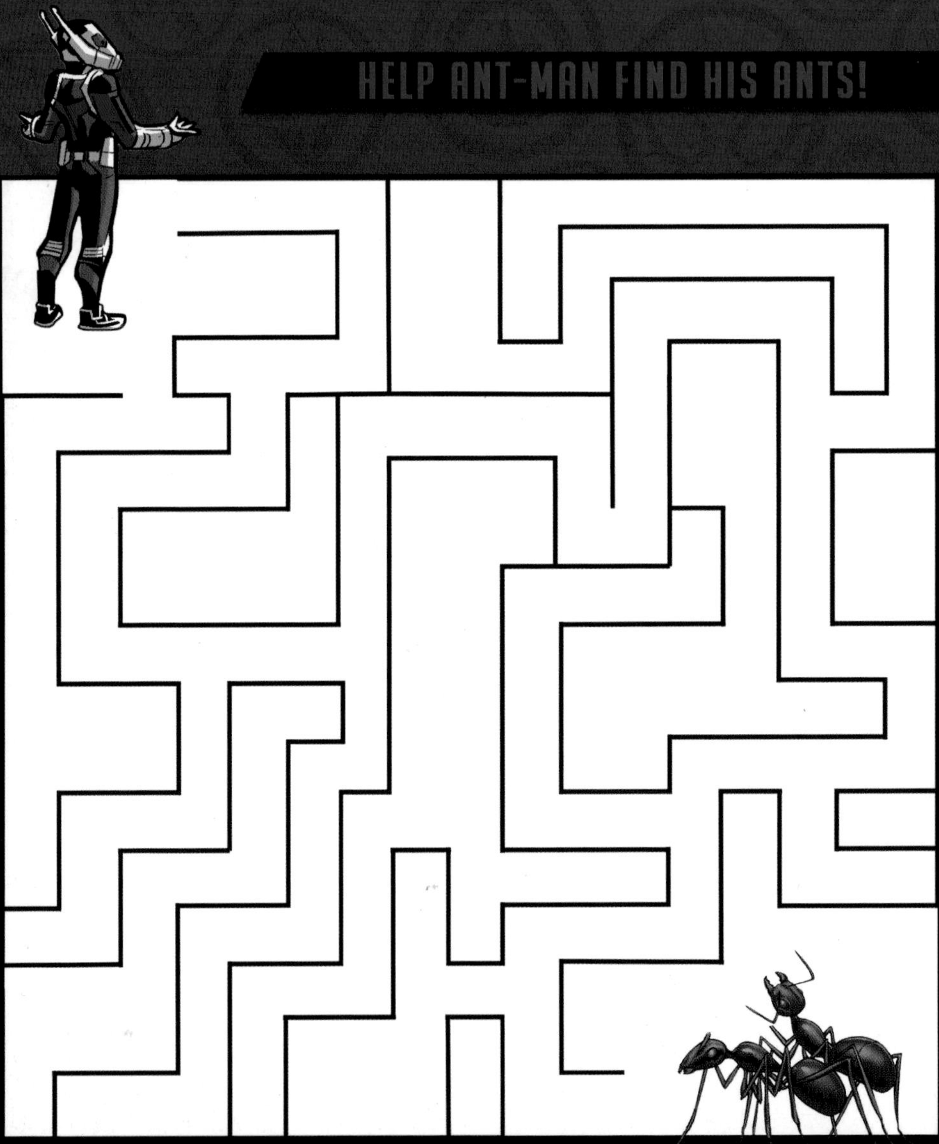

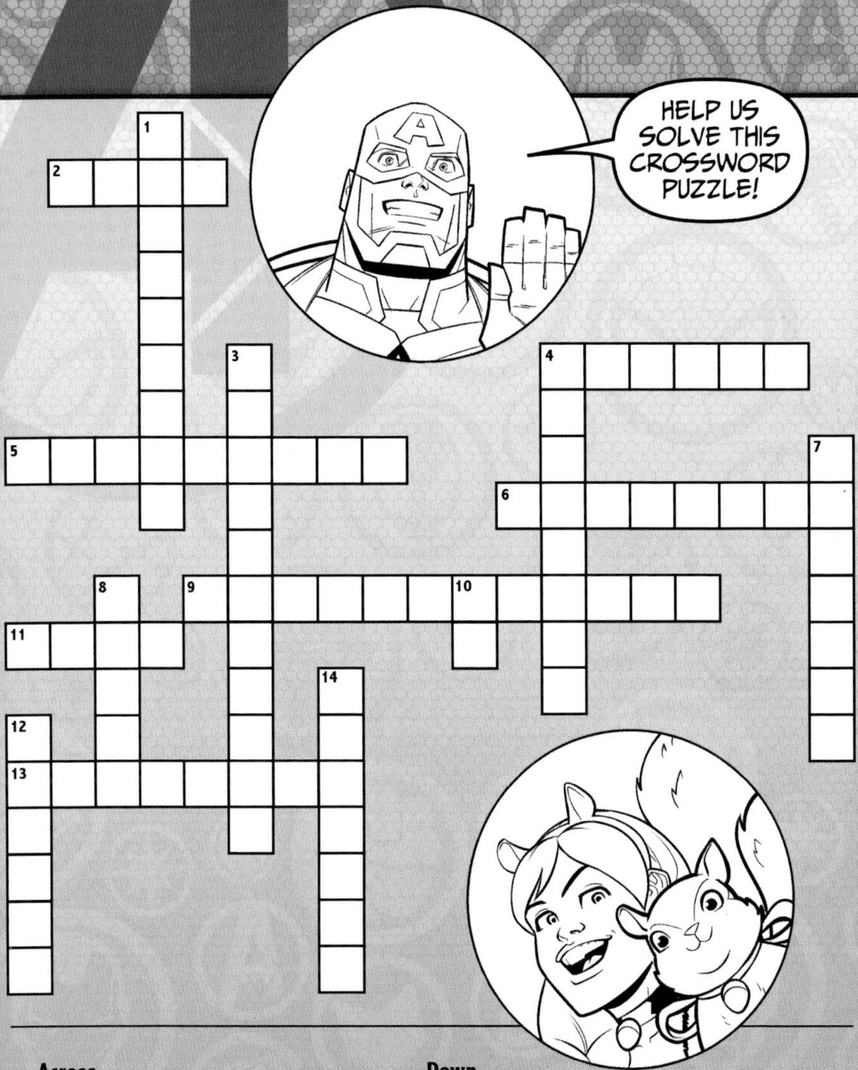
HELP US SOLVE THIS CROSSWORD PUZZLE!

Across

2. Do this at red light

4. Use this disc to protect yourself

5. Learn about a possible future profession at. (Two words)

6. Squirrel Girl's sidekick.

9. Early level of schooling.

11. Sticky material used in arts and crafts.

13. Earth's Mightiest Heroes.

Down

1. To freely help out.

3. This person drives a red truck.

4. This animal loves to eat nuts!

7. This person instructs you at school.

8. This person helps doctors in a hospital

10. Do this at a green traffic light.

12. This always comes first when doing something potentially dangerous.

14. What a super hero wears.